She stopped at the door and sent him a text. A moment later, it swung open. She did her best to keep her eyes focused on his face and not the corded muscles of his arms and chest visible beneath the sleeveless tee. Then again, with his newly trimmed mustache and beard, long eyelashes, and golden-brown-sugar eyes, his face was just as much a visual treat as the rest of his body.

Khalil's low chuckle snapped her out of her thoughts. "Come on in."

He backed up just enough so that when she passed their bodies brushed against each other, the contact sending a jolt of awareness through her. Lexia stifled a moan. Halfway across the room, she turned around and noticed him standing with his back braced against the door, arms folded. She angled her head. "What?" He straightened and came toward her with the grace of a panther and she unconsciously took a step back.

Khalil stroked a finger down her cheek. "I didn't get my hello kiss."

Before Lexia could blink, his mouth came down on hers, hot and demanding.

Dear Reader,

If you've kept up with the Gray siblings so far, you know that Khalil Gray is the most laid-back of the five, and I'll admit to being surprised by some of the things he revealed to me. But his easygoing manner is going to be put to the test, as well as his claim that there isn't a woman alive to make him give up his single status. Lexia Daniels isn't eager to lose her heart either, but life and love don't always play by our rules, as they'll soon find out. I hope you enjoy their journey because I sure did!

As always, I so appreciate all your love and support. Without you, I couldn't do this.

Much love,

Sheryl

Website: www.SherylLister.com

Email: sheryllister@gmail.com

Facebook: Facebook.com/SherylListerAuthor

Twitter: Twitter.com/1Slynne

A Touch of Love

SHERYL LISTER

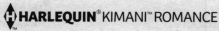 HARLEQUIN® KIMANI™ ROMANCE

Recycling programs
for this product may
not exist in your area.

ISBN-13: 978-0-373-86522-2

A Touch of Love

HARLEQUIN®
www.Harlequin.com

Printed in U.S.A.

Sheryl Lister has enjoyed reading and writing for as long as she can remember. She writes contemporary and inspirational romance and romantic suspense. She's been nominated for an Emma Award and an RT Reviewers' Choice Best Book Award, and named BRAB's 2015 Best New Author and 2016 Breakout Author and Black Pearls Magazine's 2017 Author of the Year. When she's not reading, writing or playing chauffeur, Sheryl can be found on a date with her husband or in the kitchen creating appetizers and bite-size desserts. Sheryl resides in California and is a wife, mother of three daughters and a son-in-love, and grandmother to two very special little boys. Visit her website at www.sheryllister.com.

Books by Sheryl Lister

Harlequin Kimani Romance

Just to Be with You
All of Me
It's Only You
Tender Kisses
Places in My Heart
Unwrapping the Holidays with Nana Malone
Giving My All to You
A Touch of Love

Visit the Author Profile page
at Harlequin.com for more titles.

For DeAnna Swope, because you're amazing!

Acknowledgments

My Heavenly Father, thank you for my life.
You never cease to amaze me with Your blessings!

To my husband, Lance—you continue to show me
why you'll always be my #1 hero!

To my children, family and friends—thank you for your
continued support. I appreciate and love you!

A huge thank you to Thomas Swope, Jr. and
DeAnna Swope for providing me with a small glimpse
of the Deaf Community. Your help was invaluable!
DeAnna currently serves on the Deaf Anti-Violence
Board in Georgia, is a case manager at Avita Community
Partners, and was recognized as one of the 2016 Rising
Stars: Black and Deaf Inspirations as a leader in the
community.

To my Club N.E.O. sisters—I love you ladies!

A special thank you to the readers and authors I've met
on this journey. You continue to enrich my life.

Thank you to my editor, Patience Bloom, for your
editorial guidance and support.

A very special thank you to my agent, Sarah E. Younger.
I appreciate you more than words can say.

Chapter 1

"What the hell do you mean they were charged twice?" Khalil Gray stopped in his tracks. He met the disapproving glare of a grandmotherly woman and offered up a tight smile. Lowering his voice, he repeated the question.

"I have no idea," Felicia McBride answered. The twenty-six-year-old college student worked as the assistant manager at his fitness center, Maximum Burn. "There've been four calls since you left, with members saying their accounts were debited twice this month. They've already been corrected, but I have no idea why it happened in the first place."

He ran an agitated hand down his face. "Thanks, Felicia. I'll check it out when I get back." He ended the call, still trying to figure out what was going on. He had owned the gym for five years and never had a problem before.

Khalil continued through the lobby toward the elevators and jabbed the button with more force than necessary. He toyed with stopping in Oasis Café for his favorite low fat apple cinnamon coffee cake, but because of traffic and construction across from the Wilshire District office building, he was already fifteen minutes late for the Wednesday morning staff meeting at his family's home safety company. The elevator doors opened and he stepped back to allow the stream of people to exit before boarding and riding the car up to the sixth floor.

Khalil greeted the receptionist and walked briskly down the hallway to the large conference room. He slid into a vacant seat and turned his attention to what his older brother, Brandon, was saying. Brandon had taken over as CEO of the company nine months ago. Their father, Nolan Gray, had started the company upon his discharge from the army after being disheartened by the difficulty in getting services and accommodations for the disabled. He'd decided to do something about it by designing them himself. Their father's best friend, Thaddeus Whitcomb—who had lost the lower part of his leg while serving—joined the company as a minor partner and vice president. The two men had a long-standing agreement that there would always be a Gray at the helm as CEO and a Whitcomb as vice president. Currently, only Brandon and their older sister, Siobhan, worked for the company. He listened as each department gave updates.

After the last person finished, Brandon directed his attention to Khalil. "Khalil, you're still going to be meeting with production about your equipment, right?"

Khalil nodded. "Next week. The second gym is scheduled to open in June and I don't want any delays." They had broken ground a year ago on the now three-level center, and the building would be completed in four weeks, barring any problems. He wanted all the equipment to be ready for installation.

"So, roughly three months until opening day. Let me know if you run into any difficulties. Is there anything else?"

Khalil glanced at the wall clock. It was almost eleven. Any hope he had of getting that coffee cake dissipated. When no one spoke, he pushed the chair from the table and started to stand.

"I have one quick thing."

He dropped back into his seat and groaned inwardly. He loved his sister-in-law, but couldn't she table her comments until the next meeting? Brandon had met Faith Alexander when he'd come to her rescue after a car accident. Unbeknownst to either of them, Faith was the long-lost daughter of Thaddeus Whitcomb, and rightful heir to the VP position. Uncle Thad, as they affectionately called him, had been looking for his daughter for twenty-eight years after his wife divorced him. Khalil smiled inwardly remembering all the fireworks that followed when Brandon found out the woman he had rescued and begun dating was actually going to be his second-in-command. He hadn't been too happy since he'd grown up thinking he would head the company alone—a fact that Brandon had reiterated several times. Things had worked out between Brandon and Faith and they had married six weeks ago.

Khalil tuned back in to Faith discussing the new intern program. It gave him an idea about doing something similar at the gym. A few minutes later, the meeting ended.

"Hey, Khalil. I want to talk to you before you leave."

He shot a glare at Brandon. Another five minutes passed before his brother made it over to where Khalil stood impatiently waiting.

"Why are you frowning at me like that?" Brandon asked.

"Because it's after eleven and my coffee cake is probably gone by now." He strode out of the conference room, leaving Brandon to follow. "If you want to talk, we need to do it on the way downstairs."

Brandon chuckled. "Weren't you grumbling about that three weeks ago when you were here?" He pushed the down button on the elevator.

Khalil only attended the weekly staff meeting when he had something on the agenda. "Yeah, and you'd better hope it's not all gone *again*. Dad's staff meetings never ran this long. You're taking this CEO thing way too far."

"Well, we have two new products in the design phase and have to finalize plans for our interns who'll be starting soon, so there's a lot to discuss."

When the elevator arrived, they joined four other occupants and rode down to the first floor without speaking. As soon as the doors opened, Khalil hurried across the lobby to Oasis Café. The only things left in the display case in the spot where the coffee cake usually sat were the tipped-over sign and crumbs.

Behind him, Brandon laughed softly. "Guess you'll have to get here early next time."

Before he could tell his brother where to go, a tall, pretty woman approached.

"Good morning. Table for two?" She reached for menus.

"No, thank you." Khalil pointed to the glass case. "Do you have any more of the low fat apple cinnamon coffee cake?"

"Sorry. We sold the last piece about an hour ago." She chuckled. "It's our most popular item and it goes fast. We still have some other pastries you can choose from."

He frowned. He didn't want any of those sugar-laden sweets. After spending over a decade in the modeling and fitness business, he was very selective about what went into his body. The only allowances he made were family dinners. His mother could throw down in the kitchen and he looked forward to the monthly get-togethers. "Thanks, but I'll pass."

She smiled. "Is there anything else I can get you?"

"Yes, I'll take…" Khalil trailed off when a woman wearing an apron came from the back and placed a plate on the counter. A wide headband held back her thick, wavy natural hair, and she had flawless skin, wide, dark brown eyes and lush lips, all set in an exquisite mocha face.

"I saw you this morning and knew you'd be in. You're later than usual," she said.

The deep, throaty sound of her voice caught him off guard and sent a jolt to his midsection. Khalil sent a scathing look over his shoulder at Brandon, then smiled, reached for her hand and brought it to his lips. "This is the best thing that has happened to me lately and I just may have to ask for your hand in marriage, lovely lady."

Her brow lifted and she gave him a sassy smile. "Sorry, but I only accept marriage proposals from men whose name I know."

His grin widened. "Is that right?" Was she flirting with him? She tried to pull her hand back, but he didn't let go. "Then let me introduce myself. Khalil Gray. And you are?"

Staring at him, she said softly, "Lexia. Lexia Daniels."

"So, Lexia Daniels, exactly how long do we need to know each other before you say yes to my proposal?"

Lexia shook her head and gently, but firmly withdrew her hand. "I need to get back to work." She placed a cup on the counter, along with a decaf vanilla chai tea bag—his favorite. "Enjoy your coffee cake and tea." She turned and headed back the way she'd come.

"This should improve your mood some," Brandon said.

"Mmm-hmm." Khalil had been here several times since the café reopened under new management almost two years ago and couldn't recall ever seeing her. His gaze followed the sweet curve of her hips until she disappeared.

The other woman smiled knowingly and rang up his purchases.

He handed her some bills. "Is she the chef?"

She laughed. "No, Lexia isn't the chef, though she can cook her butt off. She owns the place." She leaned forward and said conspiratorially, "But she does make that coffee cake."

Owner? Khalil was even more intrigued. He craned his neck trying to get another glimpse of Lexia, but didn't see her. "Can you ask her to come back out for a moment? I didn't get a chance to thank her."

"You bet. By the way, my name is Samantha. But you

can call me Sam." She tossed him a bold wink and strutted off.

Brandon shook his head.

"What?" Khalil asked while filling his cup with hot water. He broke off a piece of the warm cake and popped it in his mouth. Lexia must have heated it.

"I thought you were dating that model you met six months ago. How are you flirting with another woman?"

"Not dating. It's publicity."

"You said you were done with modeling and appearances."

"I am. It's for her. Rosalyn's agent and I go way back, and since she's a relative newcomer, he thought it would help her career. I promised to escort her to the fund-raiser benefiting teen models in New York next month, but that's—" He stopped short when Lexia approached. Up close, she was even shorter than he thought and he towered over her petite frame by more than a foot.

"Sam said you wanted to talk to me."

"Yes. I just wanted to thank you for the cake. You've made my day much better."

Lexia let out a short bark of laughter. "If that's all it takes to make your day—" An embarrassed expression crossed her face and she cleared her throat. "You're welcome. I'm glad you enjoy it."

"I am definitely enjoying it." And he was enjoying her. "Does this mean I can count on you to save me a slice if I'm late again?"

She averted her attention briefly to wave at a woman entering, then turned back. "I don't know when you'll be here."

Khalil moved closer. "I'll be more than happy to call and let you know."

"That's…that's not necessary," she said quickly. "Just

pop in when you arrive and Sam can set aside a piece if you don't have time to get it then." Lexia took two steps back. "Was there anything else, Mr. Gray?"

"Khalil. And no." For now. "Thanks, again."

She nodded, spun around and headed toward the booth where the woman Lexia had waved to was sitting.

He removed the tea bag, added a package of raw sugar, a dash of milk and stirred. Brandon was still staring at him. "What now?" He gestured to a nearby table and they sat.

"You seem a little preoccupied with the owner."

He grinned. "It's nothing but a little harmless flirting. She's not even my type. I prefer my women a little taller and ones who have legs that go on forever."

Brandon studied Khalil for a long moment. "She may not be the type you're used to dating, but she may end up being *exactly* your type."

Khalil waved Brandon off. "Don't get all sentimental on me now that you've gotten married. I told you before, there's not a woman alive who can make me give up my single life. After all the relationship drama I've seen over the past decade and a half…I'll pass." He acknowledged that Lexia was a beautiful woman, but that was as far as it went. Never again would he allow his emotions to overrule his good sense. "What did you want to talk to me about?"

"I noticed you on your phone and frowning during the meeting. Is everything okay?"

Khalil took a sip of tea and set the cup down. Just thinking about what Felicia told him incensed him all over again. "I got a call from my assistant manager telling me a few people have complained that they had been double charged for their membership fee this month." He continued eating.

"How did that happen?"

"Hell if I know." He polished off the last few bites. "She's already had the charges reversed, but I need to figure out why it happened in the first place."

Brandon frowned. "Strange. Well, let me know if there's something I can help with." He stood.

Khalil followed suit. "You have enough on your plate with the company and I can handle it."

"I have no doubts about that, but the offer stands."

"Thanks." He passed the table where Lexia sat with the woman. Her wide smile and sparkling eyes held him spellbound briefly and he forced himself to keep moving. Their eyes connected momentarily before she looked away and continued her conversation.

In the lobby, Brandon chuckled. "You'd better be careful, little brother or else you'll be the next one down the aisle."

Khalil snorted. "Please. I told you she's not my type. See you later." He left Brandon at the elevator and headed for the parking lot. He had been fortunate enough to grab the spot of someone leaving, which kept him from having to park in the underground garage, as he normally did. His gaze automatically shifted to the café and Lexia. No, she wasn't his type, but she did fascinate him.

Lexia Daniels tried to focus on what her best friend, Elyse Ross, was saying, but kept stealing peeks at Khalil Gray. From the way he moved and talked, to the playful glint in his light brown eyes and sexy, dark caramel body, the man was absolutely gorgeous. A few seconds later, her gaze drifted once more to the table where Khalil sat eating and talking with the other man, who she knew worked in the building. The two men favored each other and she guessed they might be brothers. Lexia could still feel the hairs of Khalil's neatly barbered close-cropped beard and soft lips grazing the back of her hand. She unconsciously rubbed the spot, trying to erase the sensation.

Elyse waved a hand in front of Lexia's face.

She blinked.

"Are you okay?"

Lexia smiled and signed back, "I'm fine." Elyse had lost her hearing as a result of a virus she'd contracted as a teen. Lexia and their other friend, Janice Hughes, had learned sign language to communicate more effectively with Elyse. "What are you doing here in the middle of the day? Don't you have a school to run?"

"Hey, when you're the boss…" Elyse shrugged. A sly smile curved her lips. "So, how long have you known that delicious specimen of a man? I saw the way he looked at you. And you can't seem to keep your eyes off him."

"I don't really know him. He comes in here every few weeks or so and orders a piece of the low fat apple cinnamon coffee cake and decaf vanilla chai tea. I assume he has business here." Lexia was usually in the back whenever he appeared and, although he couldn't see her, she never missed him. Just like always, Khalil Gray wore an expensive pair of track pants paired with an equally expensive fitted athletic shirt that showed off the lean well-defined muscles in his upper body. Clearly, he spent hours in a gym.

"Obviously you know him well enough to remember what he orders."

Lexia laughed. "It's not that hard because he's been ordering the same thing for over a year. Anyway, what's up?"

"I was going to call you last night, but I wanted to tell you this in person."

Her heart started pounding in alarm and her hands moved rapidly. "What happened? Is Sheldon okay? Did something—"

Elyse reached for Lexia's hands to still them, and then smiled. "My husband is just fine and there's nothing wrong." She placed a hand on her belly, then placed both arms together and rocked them back and forth.

Lexia's eyes lit up. She jumped out of the booth and rushed around to the other side. "You're having a baby!"

She nodded. The two women shared a hug. Once Lexia went back to her seat, Elyse wiped her tears. "The only thing that would make this perfect is if Janice was here."

She squeezed her friend's hand and they fell silent. Janice rounded out their trio. Friends since the age of ten, they'd laughed, cried and basically done life together. Janice and her two daughters had been killed in a car accident a year and a half ago, three months after Oasis Café opened. Janice's husband, Cameron, had been devastated when he lost his high school sweetheart.

As if she'd read Lexia's mind, Elyse asked, "Have you seen Cam lately? I've been so worried about him."

Lexia shook her head sadly. "He usually comes around every four or five weeks, but I haven't heard from him in close to two months." The tragedy had taken a toll on him and in the end Cameron had lost everything, including himself. "I'm praying he shows up soon."

She nodded. "When you see him, give him a hug from me."

"I will." Silence stretched between them again and she offered up a silent prayer for her friend.

Elyse slid out of the booth. "I'd better get back."

Lexia came to her feet. "Thanks for sharing your good news. Give my congratulations to Sheldon." She opened her mouth to say something else, but went still when she noticed Khalil through the window. Their eyes locked for a brief moment. He shot her a sexy grin and winked. Lexia's pulse skipped and the back of her hand tingled with remembrance of their earlier encounter. Irritated that he affected her this way, she jerked her gaze away.

Elyse laughed and shook her head. "Should I be offering you congratulations, as well?"

She frowned. "No."

"Whatever you say. We'll see if you're still spouting that nonsense the next time we talk."

"Nonsense is right. Been down that road before and I'd just as soon not go there again." Even after almost three years, the sting of her divorce still left a bitter taste in her mouth. They shared another hug, said goodbye, and Lexia went back to her office to finish her supply order.

Two hours later, she left her office and found a crowded café. Sam and the part-time server Lexia had hired were rushing from table to table as the chef barked out ready orders. She intercepted Sam. "What is going on?" The café closed at three and now, with an hour to go, the diner was more crowded than the lunch rush hour.

"There's some big meeting going on at one of the companies upstairs and this was their lunch break." Sam continued to the table carrying an armload of plates.

Lexia donned her apron and hairnet and joined the chef in the kitchen. She cooked, filled and carried plates. At two fifty-five, the last customers exited. She and Sam collapsed into the nearest booth.

"I really appreciate all the business, but my feet and arms are about to fall off," Sam said with a groan. "And we still have to clean up." Because they usually only had a few stragglers after two, they were able to clean up and prep for the next day, and be gone by three thirty. Today, it would take much longer.

Lexia chuckled. "Well, take five minutes. You deserve it."

"I'm leaving now, Lexia."

She turned to see Jayla with her backpack slung over her shoulder. "Okay. Thanks for staying a little later. You're not going to be late for school, are you?" Nineteen-year-old Jayla Howard was a sophomore at UCLA, studying biochemistry. She had come up to Lexia after a food demonstration six months ago to tell her how much she had enjoyed the dish. The two spent several minutes talking and when Jayla mentioned needing a job to supplement her financial aid, Lexia had hired her to work four hours a day.

"Nope. Class doesn't start until six, but I'm meeting my study group. I already texted to let them know I'd be a few minutes late. I'll see you tomorrow."

"Bye," Lexia and Sam chorused.

A minute passed and Sam said, "That Khalil Gray is one fine man. I can't believe you didn't give him your number."

She sighed and leaned her head against the seat. "Sam, you know what happened the last time I gave a *fine man* my number."

"I do, but he might be worth another shot. I Googled him. Want to know what I found out?"

Yes! "No," she answered, hoping she sounded disinterested.

Sam laughed. "Girl, you're not fooling me." She pushed to her feet and braced her hands on the table. "You know you want to know. And, ooh, the photos. *Sexy!*" She pulled out her phone, tapped a few buttons and fanned herself. She held the phone out to Lexia.

Lexia ignored the phone and stood. "We need to clean up so I can go home. I have some recipes to work on." The angle of the screen let her see just enough to know he was shirtless and it took everything in her not to snatch the phone and get an up close and personal view. "If you're so interested, maybe you should give him *your* number."

"I would, but he didn't ask me. Besides, I'm already dating someone." Sam glanced down at the phone again. "Mmm, mmm, mmm!"

She rolled her eyes and strode off. The temptation to see the photo was so strong, Lexia had to stop in her office and lock her phone in the drawer before returning to the front and starting on the display case. *I am not interested in that man.* His smiling face floated across her mind along with her body's reaction and she groaned inwardly. The next time he came in, she planned to stay in her office, far away from temptation.

Chapter 2

Tuesday morning, Khalil's head came up when a knock sounded on his open office door. He stood and extended his hand. "Thanks for coming, Alonzo. And so early." They'd been trying to schedule the meeting for over a week, and settled on seven this morning due to both their busy workloads. He gestured to the chair across from his desk.

Alonzo Wright gripped Khalil's hand in a firm handshake, then sat. "Sorry it took me so long to get over here. Omar said you're having some problems with your clients being overcharged?" Alonzo Wright had come highly recommended by Khalil's pro football player brother-in-law, Omar Drummond. The private investigator had been instrumental in solving a scheme to ruin both Omar and Khalil's sister Morgan's reputations orchestrated by Omar's former agent.

"No problem. I know you're busy. And, yes." He took a moment to explain the double charges. "I can't figure out for the life of me why they're happening all of a sudden. There were four last Monday when I called you and six more since then."

"Have you changed your billing system recently?"

"No. It's been the same since the day I opened the doors."

"How many people have access?"

"Three—the manager, assistant manager and me." Felicia had been with him for four years and he'd hired Logan Smith as manager a little over a year ago after his last manager relocated to another state. Khalil relayed that information to Alonzo.

Alonzo stroked his chin. "Unless someone's hacked into your system, it sounds to me like you have a virus of the two-legged variety."

He stilled. "You think it's someone who works here?" He mentally went through all five personal trainers on his staff, but dismissed them immediately. None of them would do something like this. "I haven't had any trouble with my staff, so I can't see it being one of them."

"Maybe not," Alonzo said, leaning back in the chair. "But it can't hurt to check them out. Do you mind if I look at your computer?"

Khalil stood and relinquished his chair. "By all means. Omar didn't say you were a computer whiz."

He smiled. "Just a little something I picked up along the way."

He stood off to the side while Alonzo clicked away. He rotated his head to see the wall clock. His meeting with the production manager at the home safety company wouldn't start until ten, so he had plenty of time. Today, he planned to arrive early and stop in the café. True, he wanted the cake, but he also wanted to see Lexia. Khalil hadn't been able to stop thinking about her all week and the sound of her low, throaty voice played over and over in his head. He briefly wondered what it would be like to hear her calling his name as he...

"Your system is tight, man."

The sound of Alonzo's voice snapped Khalil out of his lustful thoughts. "That's good news, isn't it?"

Alonzo chuckled. "Yes, and no. Yes, because it means there's not some nutjob out there stealing your clients' information. No, because it could mean that—"

"That there's someone here deliberately stealing money from the members," he finished.

"Exactly."

Again, Khalil tried to come up with a plausible scenario of why one of his employees would do something like this. "What do you suggest?"

He tapped a finger on the desk. "I can do a couple of things. One, I can install a program on your computer that will alert you if someone goes in and debits an account outside of the scheduled dates. I noticed that you have cameras installed outside and on both floors of the gym, but none in here. Are there any in the other offices?"

"No. It never occurred to me to put them in the offices because I don't keep much in here and I have a lock on my file cabinet and drawers."

"I'd like to install some, if you don't mind. And when no one's here."

"I don't mind at all. The gym doesn't close until midnight. I'm not open on Sunday, but I don't want to wait that long." Unless Alonzo came before five in the morning, when the gym opened, Khalil would have no choice but to wait.

Alonzo rose to his feet. "Neither do I. The quicker we get on this, the quicker your people's money will be safe. Let me check my schedule and work something out."

"I appreciate your help."

He opened the door. "I'll give you a call later today or tomorrow."

Khalil stood there for several seconds after Alonzo left. *What the hell is going on?* The intercom on his desk buzzed. He leaned over and pushed the button. "Yes."

"Khalil, Anita Crowder is here," the front receptionist said.

"Thanks. I'll be right down." Turning his mind to his client, he locked the office and went downstairs for the personal training session.

An hour and a half later, Khalil rushed back to his office to gather the drawings and reports for his meeting. His session had gone over by thirty minutes because he had to assure Anita that she would not look like the Incredible Hulk if she did some weight lifting. The woman had complained the entire session. Not until he showed her photos of other female clients he'd worked with, did she relax.

He still had an hour to get to his meeting and the drive from Fox Hills to the Wilshire District would take less than half an hour without traffic. However, with the sheer number of cars on the LA roads, that time could double. And he wanted to have plenty of time to stop in the café. He smiled. Yep, he was looking forward to seeing Lexia again.

As he'd predicted, the traffic was heavy and he made it with three minutes to spare. Khalil really hoped they'd complete whatever roadwork was being done near the building soon. It took ten minutes just to get into the parking garage. He was a stickler for time, so Lexia would have to wait.

Tuesday morning, Lexia yawned as she gently folded in chopped apples to her coffee cake batter and poured half into the prepared pan. She added crumb topping, the rest of the batter, a final layer of topping then put it, along with a second pan, into the oven. She told herself she hadn't made the additional pan just in case Khalil showed up, but it was a lie. She'd also promised herself she wasn't going to succumb to the urge to look him up on the internet and she had held up well over the past week. But curiosity got the best of her and, after washing her hands at the large double sink and drying them on a paper towel, she pulled out her cell and typed in his name.

Lexia expected a couple hundred hits but was stunned to see close to half a million. She clicked on the photo gallery and saw him in everything from shorts, T-shirt and running shoes to a tuxedo. However, the picture that had her attention was one taken a few years ago of him braced in a doorway, wearing nothing but a pair of black boxer briefs. Her gaze roamed over every perfect inch of his body, from the closely cut hair and goatee, to the slender well-defined muscles of his chest, arms, abs and thighs. He'd let the low beard grow in fully and she didn't know which look she liked better. "How on earth does he keep his body looking like this?" she murmured.

"I knew you'd be checking him out sooner or later."

She jumped and spun around. "Sam, you scared the crap out of me!" She drew in a calming breath. "Girl, you can't just sneak up on me like that. I could've hurt you."

Sam lifted a brow. "You didn't have anything in your hands except that phone and, with that fine brother on the screen I *knew* you weren't going to risk throwing it." She leaned closer to see the photo. "Mmm-hmm, I saw that one, too. He was a model."

Lexia stared at the photo. She could certainly believe that and it explained the upright posture and smooth, sexy walk. She glanced up to see Sam smiling, exited out of the page and shoved the phone back into her pocket.

"Oh don't put it away on my account. I could look at him all day. And that voice." Sam sighed dramatically.

So could she, but that's how she got caught up the last time. She didn't need another silver-tongued devil in her life. "Wait. Shouldn't you be saving all your staring for your boyfriend?"

"I'm not planning to touch. Just look and admire," she said with a grin.

"Well, you'll have to look at him on your break. We have work to do."

"Whatever you say, boss. I do think you ought to talk to him, though. It's time for you to jump on the horse again."

Lexia ignored the smirk on her friend's face. Sam had witnessed firsthand what Lexia went through with her divorce and knew Lexia had sworn off men indefinitely.

By the time they placed the muffins and other pastries

that the chef, James Willis, had made into the display case and brewed coffee, the coffee cake was done. After letting it cool for fifteen minutes, Lexia sliced it and added it to the case just as the six-thirty opening time rolled around. They had a steady stream of customers for the first couple of hours. Many people sat to eat while reading the paper or working on tablets. As soon as the rush hour died down, she retreated to her office.

An hour later, Sam stuck her head in the door. "Guess who's here, Lexi?"

By the smile on her friend's face, Lexia figured it had to be Khalil. "And? Just give him the plate you insisted we set aside *just in case*."

"I would, but he specifically asked to see you."

She lowered her head to the desk and groaned.

Sam laughed. "Hey, at least he looks good and has it going on. It could be worse."

She glared. "You're not helping, Samantha."

"Uh-oh, she called me by my whole name. Must be serious. And I am helping. No need to let your best years pass you by because of one idiot." She folded her arms and leaned against the door frame. "I still wish you had let me kick Desmond's butt."

Lexia smiled. Sam had been with her when she caught Desmond Martin and one of the waitresses who worked at the diner they owned having sex in the office. He hadn't shown one ounce of remorse and made it his mission to hurt Lexia by taking away the diner when she wouldn't "forget about it," as he'd said. Samantha, with her five-ten height, had been ready to dismember him. If Lexia thought they could get away with it, she might have. Now there was Khalil Gray. She pushed to her feet.

Sam straightened and pointed a finger Lexia's way. "And be nice."

Lexia rolled her eyes. "I'm always nice."

She burst out laughing. "Tell that to the last four guys that you sliced and diced so sweetly they're still trying to figure out what happened."

"I don't know what you're talking about," she lied. Since her divorce, she'd immediately shut down any man who had shown the least bit of interest in her—delete and block. Why she hadn't done the same thing to Khalil was a mystery. Lexia sighed heavily. "Let me go see what he wants." She walked past Sam and started toward the front.

Sam stopped her. "Ah, you might want to take this." She held out the plate.

She ignored Sam's knowing smirk, snatched the plate covered in plastic wrap and strode off. Khalil was standing with his back to her and talking on his cell when she approached and Lexia took a moment to study his slim build. He stood over six feet and gave new meaning to *fine* and *sexy*. If she had to guess by his attire, she would say he was some kind of fitness buff. Once again, he wore a pair of athletic pants, which accentuated a firm muscular butt that made her want to find out if it was as hard as it looked. She chastised herself for the errant thought and promptly shoved it aside. As if sensing her presence, he turned and smiled. Her pulse skipped. *Heart-stopping* was the only way to describe it. And those eyes. If she had any sense, she'd drop the plate on a table and get as far away from this man as fast as possible.

"I'll call you back," she heard him say. He stuck the phone in his pocket. "How are you, Lexia?"

"Fine." She handed him the plate. "S—"

"Lexi figured you'd be in and saved you an extra-large piece," Sam said as she breezed by carrying full plates, earning a scowl from Lexia.

Lexia wanted to strangle Sam. Sam knew good and well she had cut that piece herself.

Khalil's smile widened. "Thanks for looking out for me. How did you know I'd be here today?"

"I didn't." No way would she tell him she'd spotted him earlier as he rushed toward the elevator. "Well, enjoy your food."

"Aren't you going to join me?"

"I hadn't planned to. I have a lot of work to do."

He cupped her elbow and steered her toward a booth at the far end. "I'm sure Sam won't mind if you keep me company for a few minutes. After all you *are* the boss."

The warmth of his touch ignited a fluttering sensation in her stomach. To keep from melting in a puddle, Lexia quickly slid into the booth.

Khalil set the plate down. "I'll be right back."

She watched his sexy swagger as he headed back to the counter and knew, instinctively, that he'd gone back for tea. *That walk should be outlawed!* She could just imagine him strutting down a runway. She frowned when he came toward her with two cups.

"Chamomile with honey and lemon for you and, of course, decaf vanilla chai for me." He took a seat across from her and pushed the cup her way.

Lexia sent a lethal glare Sam's way. *The traitor.* "Thanks," she murmured.

"So how long have you been a chef?" he asked, starting in on his food.

"Eight years, but I've been cooking since I was a teen." She had fond memories of Mr. Wall letting her help in the kitchen of his small diner. Just as quickly, another thought stirred up the anger and hurt she had worked so hard to forget. Not wanting to dwell on the unpleasantness, she took a sip of her tea and changed the subject. "What about you? Do you work here in the building?"

Khalil finished chewing. "Lately, it's starting to feel like I work here, but no, I don't. Our family-owned home safety company is located on the sixth floor and I attend some of the meetings. I'm actually in fitness."

"I figured it was something like that by the way you're always dressed. Are you some kind of personal trainer?"

"Yes, among other things." He leaned forward and locked his gaze with hers. "Are you looking for some *personal* training?"

A vision of his hands on her demonstrating some exercise technique flashed in her mind. Lexia choked on her tea. She hastily set the cup down with a thud.

"Are you okay?"

When he started to stand, she held up a hand. "I'm fine," she croaked. "It just went down the wrong pipe." She cleared her throat, took a careful sip and swallowed without incident. "See. Fine."

Khalil studied Lexia for a moment, and then nodded. They fell silent. "You didn't answer my question."

She had hoped he'd forgotten. "No. Although I probably should work out more consistently, my schedule doesn't allow for a gym membership right now. Where do you work?"

"Maximum Burn in Fox Hills."

Great. Less than ten minutes from my condo. "I've heard of it."

"Anytime you want to come by, let me know."

"Um…I heard it's pretty pricey."

He waved her off. "We offer plans to fit every budget. I don't want money to be an obstacle for anyone looking to maintain or start a healthy lifestyle. But you don't have to be concerned about money. For you, the cost is free."

Lexia narrowed her eyes. "What's the catch?"

Khalil laughed. "No catch. Well, maybe a small one."

"I knew it."

He reached for her hand. "A date. Next Tuesday morning, you and me, right here in this booth, ten thirty."

She should have known better than to ask. From the moment they had met, he'd made his interest clear. "I don't—"

"It's a win-win for both of us. I get to spend more time with a beautiful lady and you get three free personal training sessions. And before you say you don't have time to go to the gym, I'll design a program for you that can easily be done at home with just a few simple *and* inexpensive pieces of equipment. So what do you say?"

He unleashed that mesmerizing smile on her and Lexia heard herself agreeing.

"Great. It's a date. You can let me know next time what your fitness goals are and when you'd like to start your sessions."

She made a move to stand and he was up and around to her side with his hand extended in a flash. She tentatively placed her hand in his and he helped her to her feet. "Thanks."

Once again, he brought her hand to his lips. "Until next week, Lexia." He smiled, winked and strolled out.

What in the world have I gotten myself into?

Chapter 3

Monday evening, Lexia leaned against the kitchen counter trying to decide which recipe to use for the cooking demonstration next month. With summer fast approaching, people would most likely be looking for something a little healthier. Her mind automatically shifted to Khalil and his personal training offer. If her body reacted just from him simply holding her hand, no way could she handle a session with him standing so close, his hands roaming over her arms, sliding down her torso and hips, around to her… She abruptly halted her lustful thoughts. "Get a grip, girl," she muttered. "Recipes…that's all you're supposed to be thinking about." She flipped through the cards and lingered over one featuring shrimp tacos with a creamy cilantro sauce. *This could work.*

She searched through the cabinets and refrigerator and found all the ingredients. Lexia made a practice of shopping every week and kept her kitchen well stocked. Since it was relatively early, she decided to make homemade corn tortillas instead of using the store-bought ones. She defrosted the shrimp, removed the tails and seasoned them with a rub made from seasoned salt, pepper, cumin, paprika and chili powder, then skewered them. Next, she went to work on the cilantro sauce. Just as she finished, her phone rang. She quickly washed and dried her hands and ran to catch it. Seeing Samantha's name on the display, she said, "What's up, girlfriend?"

"Hey, girl," Samantha said. "Aaron has to work late tonight and I was wondering if you wanted to grab a bite to eat."

Lexia smiled. "Oh, so now you have time for me," she

teased. Since Samantha and Aaron started dating four months ago, Lexia and Sam rarely hung out during the week.

"Whatever. We'll see if you have time once you and Mr. Gray start hanging out."

"Yeah, right. We won't be *hanging out*. The man has *playboy* written all over him. You saw him. Besides, I'm sure he has tons of women running after him already. Remember he was a model." Against her better judgment, she'd read more about him and found out that he had modeled all over the United States and in several other countries. There had been thousands of photos of him with an array of beautiful women, and in some of the shots, they seemed quite cozy.

"Mmm-hmm, I saw him, all right. Saw that he only had eyes for you."

"You were asking about dinner."

Sam laughed. "You can change the subject, but you can't change Khalil Gray's blatant attraction to you. Now, regarding dinner, I can pick something up and bring it over or we can meet up somewhere."

"Actually, I'm experimenting with a recipe, shrimp tacos with a cilantro cream sauce on homemade corn tortillas."

"Say no more. I'll be there in fifteen minutes."

Lexia heard a beep. "Sam?" She pulled the cell away from her ear and glanced down at the display. Sam had hung up. She chuckled, shook her head and continued preparing dinner.

Twenty minutes later, she opened the door to Sam.

Sam held up a bag. "I stopped and got our favorite Moscato."

"In that case, come on in." They both laughed.

She followed Lexia to the kitchen. "Do you need me to do anything?"

"If you can grill the shrimp while I make the tortillas, that would be great."

"Sure." Sam washed her hands, then carried the plate with the shrimp skewers to the stove. She laid them on the preheated built-in grill. "Mmm, this smells so good. What spices did you use?"

Lexia rattled off the list while pressing the tortillas. When she finished, she heated the comal and added the tortillas, one at a time. Once everything was done, Lexia added some of the sauce to the shredded cabbage and mixed it in. "All right, let's try this." They fixed their plates, filled glasses of wine and sat at the kitchen table.

Sam rubbed her hands together. "I'm starving." She bit into a taco, chewed and groaned. "Oh my goodness, Lexi, this is absolutely *divine*. And this sauce." She spooned more onto her half-eaten taco. "It's so light, like a summer day. What's in it?"

"That's what I was going for. It's light sour cream, cilantro, lime and a dash of salt. I'm planning to do this for the cooking demonstration at the food festival next month." She was pleased by the outcome and agreed that the light dish would be perfect for summer.

"Girl, I hope you're planning to make at least a hundred of these because folks are going to be lined up for miles to get one. This would be a great recipe to add to the menu at the café."

"Maybe." She had been thinking about adding a few calorie-conscious items to the menu, especially since the low fat coffee cake seemed to be such a hit. One woman had called it guilt-free indulgence. "What do you think of adding three or four healthy dishes so people have options?"

"With the fitness craze going on, I think it's a great idea." Sam sipped her wine and added slyly, "I'm sure

Khalil would appreciate it. Who knows, he might start coming in for breakfast *and* lunch."

Lexia took a big gulp of wine. As much as she tried to deny it, the prospect of seeing Khalil sent a thrill through her. What would he think of the tacos?

"See, you're over there thinking about him."

Busted, she picked up a stray shrimp and popped it in her mouth. "No, I'm not," she lied. "I was thinking about what other dishes would work well." The smile on Sam's face said she knew better, but she didn't comment.

"Are you ready for your date tomorrow?"

"It's not really a date."

"That's not what he told me on his way out last week when he asked me to make sure to set aside *two* pieces of that coffee cake. You might want to redo your twist out and wear something cute."

Lexia groaned and rose from the table with her plate. "He's coming to my job, so he'll have to settle for my work clothes. If he wants anything else, he might want to find one of those models he's used to."

Yet, hours after Sam left, Lexia found herself searching through her wardrobe for something other than her normal khakis and pullover knit top.

By the time she made it in to work the next morning, Lexia was in a foul mood. She'd spent a restless night dreaming about a man she had no business even *thinking* about. Her life was simple and uncomplicated and she wanted it to stay that way. She decided that today's "date" would be the last one, no matter how much Khalil affected her.

"Lexia, there's a guy outside asking for you," Jayla said, poking her head in the office.

Her gaze flew to the clock on the wall. He was twenty

minutes early. Sighing inwardly, she came to her feet. "Thanks, Jayla. I'll be out in a moment."

"Okay." She disappeared.

Lexia drew in a calming breath, rehearsed her I-can't-see-you-again speech in her head and went out front. A relieved smile lit her face at the sight of Cameron standing outside the café. She stopped to give a meal order to Mr. Willis, then pushed through the doors. "Cam, I'm so glad to see you."

"Hey, Lexi." She could hear the sadness and fatigue in his voice.

"You want to come in and eat?"

Cameron shook his head. "Too dirty."

She scanned him from head to toe. His hair was matted and littered with pieces of lint, the shirt and jeans looked like the same ones he'd had on when she saw him last and she suspected he hadn't bathed since then, either. But beneath the dirt and grime was a good-looking man with a heart of gold. "How about we go sit on the bench outside and talk. I'll bring you some breakfast."

He nodded and shuffled out the glass doors leading to the back parking lot.

Lexia waited to make sure he was seated before going to get his food. She had to figure out a way to help him. A few minutes later, she joined him on the bench and handed him the to-go carton filled with scrambled eggs, potatoes with onions and peppers, bacon, sausage, two biscuits and a large cup of orange juice. He dived in like a starved man and her heart constricted. "How've you been? I was worried when you didn't come by last month."

Cameron shrugged and continued eating. When he finished and set the carton aside, he sighed heavily. "Thanks, Lexi." He stared out at a spot in the sky. "Jan is probably cussing me out from heaven over the mess I've made of my life."

Lexia laughed softly. "No doubt she is. But she'd also understand. Just like she was your world, you were hers." She handed him the framed photograph he had asked her to keep.

He ran his hands lovingly over the faces of Janice and their two daughters, five-year-old Lauren and one-year-old Sienna. "I miss them so much." His voice cracked.

She felt her own emotions rising and covered his hand with hers. "I know. So do I. But Jan would want you to go on."

He swiped at the tears coursing down his cheeks. "You're right and I've been thinking on it."

It was the first time in over a year he had mentioned trying to reintegrate into society on his own. Every time Lexia had brought it up in the past, he'd change the subject or leave. "If there's anything you need me to do, *anything*, just ask. Like I told you before, you're welcome to stay in the back room of the café until you get on your feet." She had added a bed months ago, hoping he would take her up on the offer.

He stared off again. "Let me think about it, okay?"

"Sure. You want to take a shower? I still have the clothes you asked me to keep."

Cameron looked down at himself. "I guess I don't smell too good."

She chuckled. "*That's* an understatement."

For the first time in almost two years, a slight smile appeared on his face. "I can always depend on you to tell me the truth."

"Always." They stood and she embraced him. When she stepped back, her gaze locked with Khalil's. He stood inside with his arms folded and a glare on his face. She glared right back.

"Friend of yours?" Cameron asked.

"Um...not really. He's just someone who frequents the café." She glanced over her shoulder. Khalil hadn't moved from the spot and his expression remained the same. *Here we go.*

Khalil finished his meeting early and had hoped to spend the extra time with Lexia, but stopped short upon seeing her outside with a large, unkempt man. His protective nature kicked into high gear. He stood there watching for a good five minutes and, when she saw him, she sent a hostile look his way. She could glare all she wanted to, but he wasn't moving until she came back inside. The man disappeared around the back of the building and Lexia entered through the glass doors and came toward him.

"You should be careful of the company you keep," Khalil said when she reached him.

"The company I keep is just fine." Lexia eyed him. "Present company excluded."

His brow lifted. "No need to get all upset. I'm just concerned about your safety. He could've been dangerous." The huge man could have easily overpowered her.

She placed a hand on her hip and scowled up at him. "Are you always so arrogant and judgmental?"

He angled his head thoughtfully. He really had upset her. A small knot of people viewed their exchange curiously. Not wanting to draw any more attention, he gently steered her toward the café.

She snatched her arm away. "What are you doing?"

Khalil grasped her hand. "People are staring. Let's go sit inside and you can tell me all about my arrogant and judgmental self." He escorted her over to the same booth they'd sat in previously.

Lexia sat across from him with her lips tightly pursed.

Having her angry with him didn't sit well. "I don't consider myself to be arrogant and judgmental, and I apologize for upsetting you. Like I said, I was only concerned about your safety."

Some of the anger drained from her face. "I wasn't in any danger. He's a friend."

"What happened to him?"

"He lost his wife and children in a car accident about a year and a half ago."

"Damn," he whispered.

"Right. So, before you go forming an opinion about someone, you should get all the facts first."

Khalil heard the censure in her voice. He had never been one to pass judgment on someone without even hearing his or her side and wondered why he had been so quick to jump to conclusions this time. "You're right." Her surprised expression prompted him to ask, "What? I don't have a problem admitting when I'm wrong."

Lexia studied him a moment, as if searching for the truth. "I'm glad to hear it."

He smiled. "So, can we start our date now?"

She shook her head and chuckled. "You don't let up for a moment, do you?"

"And risk some other guy snatching you up first? Nah." He winked and signaled the hostess. Lexia rolled her eyes and he laughed.

While eating a few minutes later, Lexia said, "I thought you didn't come here often."

"I usually don't, but I'm designing some specialized equipment for the gym and having it made and produced by my family's company."

She frowned and broke off a small piece of coffee cake. "How does that fit with home safety?"

Khalil smiled. "Since I started designing the equipment three years ago, they added a small extension to the company." When a few of his personal clients mentioned the difficulties they had using some of the machines, he transformed a section of the gym to accommodate those who were in wheelchairs, had limbs amputated or other disabilities. The new equipment would have braille and he had just installed a section of flooring that had the same feel as a mat, but without the uneven surface for those with low vision or blindness. As he had told Lexia, he didn't want any barriers for people wanting to work out.

"Wait. Do you *own* the gym?"

"Yep." He sipped his tea.

"Was that before or after mod—?" Lexia stopped midsentence and picked up her cup.

Khalil placed his cup on the table and observed her. If she knew about the modeling, she had obviously looked him up. "After."

"I...um...I wasn't stalking you or anything."

"Actually, I'm flattered."

"How did you get into modeling?"

"A couple of my high school friends dared me to enter one of those model search contests." He shrugged. "I won, so..."

She laughed. "I bet they were shocked. I guess it worked out for you by all the photos—"

"I'm glad to know you were thinking about me because I definitely thought about you." He reached for her hand. "All week long." He couldn't remember the last time a woman had invaded his dreams, but this petite fireball had not only entered them, but also consumed every corner of his mind each night.

Lexia withdrew her hand. "Khalil, I don't think this is a good idea."

"Why not? Are you saying you don't like my company?" he asked, referencing her earlier comment.

She slanted him a look. "Your company is fine…for now. But…"

Khalil's cell rang and interrupted whatever he planned to say. He pulled out the phone to check the display and cursed under his breath. It was his assistant manager. "Can you excuse me a minute, Lexia? I have to take this. I won't be long."

"Sure."

He slid out of the booth and answered while heading out to the lobby. "Hey, Felicia."

"Hi, Khalil. You asked me to call if I noticed anything regarding the charges and I thought you'd like to know that I saw Logan going into your office. I asked what he was doing and he said you asked him to check something on the computer."

He shoved the front doors open and stepped out onto the sidewalk. "Logan knows damn well I never told him to enter my office," he said through clenched teeth. He mentally retraced his morning. Had he been so anxious to leave that he forgot to lock the door? He always kept it secure when he wasn't there.

"I thought the same. That's why I called."

"Is he still there?" With the noise coming from traffic and the road construction, he stuck a finger in his ear to hear her better.

"No. He went to lunch. He didn't get a chance to log on to your computer because I busted him as soon as he went in. After he walked out, I locked your door."

Khalil paced in front of the building. Thank goodness Alonzo had come in to install the cameras last week. Khalil would be able to see exactly what Logan had been up to. "Thanks, Felicia. I'll check it out when—" A loud explosion sounded and before he could turn around, he was pitched backward and airborne.

Khalil came to lying on the ground. Every inch of his body hurt, he had difficulty breathing and there was a loud ringing in his ears. He tried to get up, but the pain forced him back down. He moaned. He could see glass and debris everywhere and people scrambling for cover. He closed his eyes as another wave of pain hit.

"Khalil! Are you okay?"

He felt someone touch him and looked up to find Lexia on her knees next to him.

She palmed his face. "Where are you hurt?"

His eyes widened, his heart raced and his chest tightened. Her mouth was moving, but he heard not one sound. He lifted his head and scanned the area—flashing lights from police vehicles, people still running, cars, but he didn't hear anything. "I can't hear you," he said, panicking. He grabbed her hand. "I can't hear you," he said again. But he didn't even hear his own voice.

Chapter 4

Lexia scanned her surroundings. Thick smoke filled the air, a large hole sat in the center of the street and nearby buildings were damaged, including the one housing her café. Her front window had been shattered, as well as several other ones in the building. She saw a few injured people being tended to and wondered if anyone had been killed. Since it was midmorning, most people were working. Had it been an hour later, things would have been much worse. She turned her attention to Khalil, who lay with his eyes closed. Lexia toyed with trying to get him up and inside, but every movement seemed to increase his pain and she didn't want to cause him further injury.

Khalil opened his eyes. "Lexia, I can't hear anything."

Although he tried to hide it, Lexia saw it for a split second. Fear. She assumed the blast had damaged his hearing and prayed it was temporary. She sensed his fear rising and placed her hand gently on his chest. She used the other one to turn his face toward her and mouthed, "You're going to be okay." He placed his hand over hers on his chest and she leaned down and placed a soft kiss on his lips. Khalil stared up at her with a strange look on his face and, belatedly, she realized what she had done. Before she could analyze it, people began streaming from the building and she caught the gaze of his brother. Lexia waved at him.

His eyes widened when he noticed Khalil and he pushed through the crowd. He dropped to his knees in his expensively tailored slacks, concern evident in his face. "Khalil, are you okay? Where are you hurt?"

Lexia laid a hand on his arm. "He can't hear you."

He whipped his head around. "What do you mean he can't hear me?"

"The blast. I think it damaged his hearing. He told me he couldn't hear anything."

He cursed and whipped out his cell phone. He snapped at a 911 operator who, apparently, wasn't responding to his satisfaction. "Well, how long is it going to take? My brother is lying in the *street* injured."

Lexia understood where he was coming from. She felt just as helpless. Finally, four fire trucks and a number of paramedics descended on the scene. "They're here."

He glanced up, mumbled something that sounded like a thank-you and disconnected the call. "I'll be right back." He stood.

"Brandon." Khalil tried to sit up and moaned again.

Brandon stopped and placed a hand on Khalil's shoulder. "Whoa. Don't try to get up." He turned to Lexia. "Make sure he doesn't move."

She nodded.

Khalil rolled his head in her direction. "Brandon is bossy as hell," he whispered. "I don't have to hear to know what's he's about to do. Don't let him piss off the paramedics. Otherwise, they'll leave me lying on this sidewalk all damn day."

Lexia smiled and nodded. She glanced up in time to see Brandon pointing in their direction and standing over the paramedic, with a heavy scowl—just as Khalil predicted—until the man followed. She and Brandon moved off to the side while the medic assessed Khalil.

A moment later, another medic joined them with a gurney. The first one spoke to Brandon. "By his shallow breathing and pain when I barely press on the area, I'd say he has a couple of broken ribs."

"And he can't hear," Lexia added.

"Thanks," the medic said. "I'll make sure to let them

know at the hospital." He nodded to the other paramedic and they carefully transferred Khalil to the gurney.

Brandon stepped forward. "I'm coming with him."

His tone and the look on his face let Lexia know he wouldn't take no for an answer. Apparently the paramedic realized it, as well, and nodded.

"Are you coming?"

She glanced over at Khalil then up at Brandon. As much as she wanted to go, Lexia didn't think it was her place. "No. But can you please let me know how he's doing?"

"I will. Thanks for being here with him." He laid a gentle hand on her shoulder, then left.

She wrapped her arms around her middle and watched as they loaded Khalil into the ambulance and drove off.

"Is he going to be okay?"

Lexia turned at the sound of Sam's voice. "I think so. But the blast damaged his ears. He can't hear."

Sam brought her hand to her mouth. "Oh no."

She recalled the split second of vulnerability she'd seen and her emotions swelled once more.

"Come on, Lexi. I'm sure he'll be okay."

Lexia took one last glance around and nodded. On the way, she spied Khalil's phone. She had no problems recognizing it because of the distinctive custom case featuring his gym's logo. She picked it up and brushed off the debris. Other than a few cracks on the face, the phone seemed to be intact. Inside, she froze upon seeing Cameron sweeping up glass from the shattered window. Tears welled in her eyes. This was the man she knew—clean shaven, low-cut hair and neatly groomed appearance. He had on a pair of black khakis and a gray polo shirt.

Cameron paused with the broom. "You good, Lexi?"

"Yeah. You clean up nicely."

He grinned. "I knew you were going to say that." He

shook his head and resumed the task, along with James, who had come out of the kitchen to help with the cleanup.

Jayla held up her phone. "It says it was a natural gas explosion. Two workers were killed and several others injured." She looked down at the screen and read for a moment, then added, "This one is considered mild and could have been much worse."

Lexia grabbed a towel and a trash bag and joined Samantha in clearing glass off the tables. She sighed. Mild or not, it would take a lot of work to repair the businesses damaged, including her own. Her heart went out to the families of the two workers and the rest of the people who had been injured. Automatically, her thoughts shifted to Khalil and how he was doing. It dawned on her that she hadn't given Brandon her number and would most likely have to wait until he came to work tomorrow to find out any information. *If* he came in. She should have gone to the hospital.

Khalil slowly came awake, glanced around the room and saw his entire family. It took a moment before everything came rushing back and he realized he was lying in a hospital bed. He moved and pain shot through his midsection. He must have made a sound because his mother crossed the room in two strides and ran her hands critically over his face. His head throbbed, the loud ringing in his ears hadn't stopped, his chest felt like someone was standing on it every time he breathed deeply—and he still couldn't hear a sound. Khalil scanned their concerned faces. "I'm all right, Mom." He frowned and gently pushed her hand away from the bandage on his temple. He saw all their mouths moving and an overwhelming sense of frustration surged inside him. Brandon raised his hand and got their attention and said something. Brandon obviously told them about Khalil's hearing loss because all eyes turned Khalil's way and his mother and two sisters, Siobhan and Morgan, started crying and rushed over to the bed. Even Faith had tears in her eyes. His father looked stricken.

Khalil leaned back against the pillows and closed his eyes. *This is all I need right now.* He couldn't stand to see them cry and bit back the urge to tell them all to leave. He sent his brothers and brothers-in-law a pleading glance. They gathered their wives, and together with his parents exited, leaving only his younger brother, Malcolm.

Malcolm pulled a chair close to the bed and sat. For the first few minutes, the pro football running back said nothing as if he knew Khalil needed a moment.

"I never could stand to see them cry."

Malcolm took out his phone, typed something and handed it to Khalil.

He read: "Neither can I. What do you need me to do? Oh, and you should probably lower your voice." Because he couldn't hear himself, Khalil had no idea how to modulate his voice. "Is this better?" he asked in what he hoped was a softer sound.

He nodded.

"Did the doctor say how long I'd be like this?"

Malcolm took the phone, typed again and handed it back.

"Brandon said the doctor told him your eardrums were ruptured from the blast and the hearing loss could last a few days, months or, depending on the damage, longer. He mentioned referring you to a specialist."

Khalil dropped the phone on his lap and cursed. What if his hearing didn't come back? He couldn't be deaf *forever*. The thought of never hearing his favorite song on the radio, the waves crashing against the shore while standing on his balcony or the laughter around the table at his family's monthly dinners made the same panic he'd felt while lying on the sidewalk come back full force. He passed the phone back to his brother, who began typing again. Was there more? He knew about the broken ribs, slight concussion and sprained wrist, thanks to a nurse who had written the information down for him while in emergency. Khalil couldn't imagine what else could be wrong and wasn't sure he wanted to know.

Malcolm stood and held the phone close enough for Khalil to read.

The gym. He had totally forgotten about it. "Yeah, I do need you to go over. I've been having some problems with some of the members being double charged." Like Khalil, Malcolm had a degree in kinesiology and the two had discussed the possibility of him joining Khalil in the business once he retired from football. He filled Malcolm in on the meeting with Alonzo and his latest phone call with Felicia. "Can you call Alonzo and have him download the images on the camera and check my computer?" Another thought occurred to him. He'd been in the middle of the call with his assistant manager and she probably had no idea what had happened. He didn't even know what happened to his phone. "Ask Felicia to cancel all my clients and tell her not to come up here. I'm fine." Not exactly the truth, but he didn't want another person staring at him with a look of pity. His family had done enough of that. "I'll contact her in a few days. Oh, and my phone is gone."

He nodded, typed something else and held up the phone. "Don't worry about your phone right now. We'll get you one when you get home."

Before Khalil could respond, a middle-aged man wearing scrubs and a white jacket, a doctor he assumed, entered carrying what looked like two cell phones.

Malcolm touched Khalil on his uninjured shoulder, pointed toward the door and mouthed, "I'm leaving."

After his brother left, the doctor pressed a few buttons on the gadgets, then handed one to Khalil. Khalil had been correct about it being a cell phone. He glanced up to see the doctor talking and started to get frustrated until the man pointed at the phone in Khalil's hand. He shifted his gaze and saw the words automatically being typed on the screen as the doctor talked.

The man introduced himself as Dr. Moyer, the ear, nose and throat specialist and asked several questions before examining Khalil's ears. "Both eardrums have been perforated. The tear in the right ear is slightly larger than the left."

After reading the information, Khalil asked, "So, how long will it take for my hearing to return?"

Dr. Moyer shrugged. "Most times the eardrums heal themselves within a few weeks and your hearing will get back to normal. But sometimes it doesn't."

"And if it doesn't?"

"Then they may need to be surgically repaired."

"And this will guarantee my hearing will return?"

The doctor shook his head. "I can't guarantee to what degree your hearing will return, or if it will at all. We just have to wait and see."

He didn't even want to think about not being able to hear again or surgery. "How long before you determine whether I have to have surgery?"

"If your hearing hasn't returned in three months, we'll reevaluate our next steps. In the meantime, you'll need to make sure no water gets in them. I'm going to prescribe an antibiotic eardrop to help protect from infections and I want you to make an appointment with my office so we can get you some information on resources."

Khalil groaned and closed his eyes. He didn't have time for this. He had too much to do with the new gym opening in three months, the renovations at the current one and the mess with the members. He sensed the doctor moving closer and opened his eyes. He lifted the phone and followed the words on the screen. "No, I don't have any other questions." Nothing other than why couldn't the man fix the problem right now, instead of waiting?

Brandon poked his head in the door and Khalil waved him in. Not like he'd leave anyway. Khalil was certain Brandon had seen the doctor enter and waited as long as he could. Although marriage had mellowed his big brother somewhat, his intense nature still hovered below the surface. Khalil watched as the doctor and Brandon talked. He assumed Dr. Moyer was sharing the same details he'd given Khalil. Brandon seemed particularly interested in the speech-to-text app and Khalil could see the wheels turning in his brother's head.

Dr. Moyer handed Khalil a card. "Here's my card. You can email me with any questions. I know this is a big change, but there's no reason you can't continue living a full, productive life." He pointed to the phones. "I'll leave these here for you and your family."

Khalil nodded. "Thanks."

As soon as the doctor closed the door, Brandon said, "This is so cool. I'm going to talk to Justin and have him check this out. He may be able to design a better app."

He rolled his eyes. *Just like I thought.* Always business. Their brother-in-law, Justin Cartwright, had partnered with Gray Home Safety to market his in-home alert system. The system sent real-time data to a smartphone letting the user know whether a door had been opened, a stove had been left on or if there had been no movement in the house for an extended period. The product gave peace of mind to families whose aging parents wanted to continue living independently. "Did that doctor not just tell you I may not ever get my hearing back? Who cares about that damn app right now? Why does everything have to be about business with you?" Khalil blew out a frustrated breath.

Brandon studied Khalil a long moment, then picked up the phone the doctor had left on the bedside tray. "That's not what he said at all. He said it could heal in a few weeks. In the meantime, you have the equipment for your new gym to finish designing, as well as overseeing the opening to keep you busy. You know we'll all help."

"How in the hell am I supposed to do that? I can't hear a damn thing! I don't want to depend on anybody driving me everywhere I go, or have everybody write down whatever they want to say all the time. I can't live like this," he gritted out. He sat up abruptly and pain shot through his ribs like a crack of lightning, slapping him back down. Khalil cursed. He clenched his fists and took several shallow breaths. It took several moments for the agony to subside.

Brandon's calm expression hadn't changed. "Are you done?" He paused for a beat. "Khalil, you are one of the smartest people I know. You learned Spanish and French when you had those modeling gigs in Spain and France, earned two degrees while traveling around the globe and single-handedly turned a gym that was folding under the previous owners into one of the best around. Your right hand is sprained, not your left. I don't know anything about the driving laws, but none of us have a problem taking you wherever you need to go, if necessary. As far as communication…" Brandon held up the device. "Done. Now, Mom and Dad are out there and anxious to get back in here. If you don't want Mom insisting you move in with them after you leave this hospital, I suggest you get yourself together, little brother."

Khalil wanted to punch something. But he knew his brother was right. Khalil was thirty-three and had been living on his own since age eighteen, but that wouldn't mean a thing if his mother thought for one moment that he couldn't manage on his own. "Fine. Give me a second before you let them in."

Minutes later, his parents rushed in behind Brandon. The frown on her face and the rapid movement of her mouth gave Khalil the impression that she was fussing at Brandon. Brandon gave him a look that said, "I told you."

Brandon showed their parents how to work the speech app and his mother took it and rushed over to the bed.

"How are you feeling, baby? Do you need me to get you anything? Where does it hurt? Do I need to have the nurse bring you something for the pain? Don't worry, when you're released, you can stay with us for a couple of weeks until you're back on your feet."

The words flew across the screen so fast there were no spaces between the questions. "Mom…" The questions continued. "Mom." He reached up and gently pried the thing out of her hand. "Mom." She glared at him. "I'm okay. I do *not* need to stay with you and Dad. I'll be fine in my own home." Or so he hoped. But, then again, he wouldn't even know if the phone or doorbell rang, or hear his alarm in the mornings. He sighed inwardly.

Over the next half hour, all his siblings came in and out of the room and his mother continued to hover. He appreciated their love and support, but the only thing he wanted was to be alone and prayed that when he woke up in the morning, he'd be able to hear again.

Chapter 5

Thursday morning, Lexia wrapped up her meeting with the contractor hired to repair the broken windows and hurried over to where Brandon stood near the cash register. From the navy tailored suit he wore today, she assumed he was on his way to work. When he stopped by yesterday, he had on sweatpants and a long-sleeved tee. He'd told her that Khalil had a rough first night and hadn't taken the news about his hearing well. She couldn't imagine what he felt, but remembered the same thing happening to Elyse. Her friend had cried for weeks, became depressed and withdrew from everyone and everything.

"Hi, Brandon. How is he?"

Brandon shook his head. "Same. He won't eat and is pretty much ignoring everybody except our parents. He may be pissed off, but not enough to risk Mama's wrath," he added with a wry chuckle.

"This is going to be a huge adjustment for him and he just needs a little time." She wanted to go see him so badly, but held back from asking.

"I guess." He scrubbed a hand down his face. "Maybe you should take him a piece of that coffee cake he's always raving about. I bet he'd eat that."

Lexia smiled. "If you're visiting him today, I can put a slice aside for you to pick up on your way out. We close up at three, but I'll be here until about four thirty or five."

Brandon angled his head thoughtfully. "I think it would be better if you delivered it yourself."

"I…um…" True, she wanted to see Khalil, but what would he think about her showing up at the hospital?

He smiled. "Yeah. That would be perfect." He glanced down at the expensive gold watch on his arm. "I have a couple of meetings this morning, but I can leave around one thirty to make a quick visit. The lunch rush is pretty much over by then, right?"

"For the most part, yes," she answered slowly.

"Is there a problem with you being gone for an hour or so?"

Her eyes widened when she realized where the conversation was headed. "Well, no, but—"

"Great. I'll stop by and drive you over. That way you won't have to worry about figuring out where to go once you reach the hospital." He took another quick peek at his watch. "I'll see you around one thirty. And thanks." He spun on his heel and strode out the door toward the elevator.

Lexia stood there stunned, wondering what just happened.

"So should I go cut that piece for you, Lexi?"

She spun around and met Sam's smiling face. "I am not talking to you."

Sam laughed and brought a hand to her heart. "Why? I didn't do anything."

"Exactly. Why didn't you say something?"

"Something like what?"

Lexia threw up her hands. "I don't know…*something*. Since you were over here eavesdropping, I'm sure you heard what his brother said about Khalil ignoring everybody. Besides, I can't just up and leave."

Sam folded her arms. "Sure you can. You do it all the time to pick up supplies or run some other errand. And, yes, I did hear what he said. But, like Brandon—that is his name, right?"

She nodded.

"Like Brandon, I believe you're exactly the person Khalil needs to see. One, the man is clearly interested in you. Two, you make the best guilt-free coffee cake anywhere. And, three, you know precisely how to deal with someone who's lost their hearing." She smiled and shrugged. "And if you don't know what to say, I'm sure Elyse will be happy to help you." She sighed. "Look, I know you're nervous about starting up with another man, but just think of this as helping a friend for now."

"I guess," Lexia mumbled. Sam was right. It was just helping a friend. Although, she wouldn't really say they were friends since she'd only known him a couple of weeks. "Well, I need to get some work done before then."

Her smile widened. "You can save all the hot stuff for when he's better."

She ignored Sam, rounded the counter and started toward the back.

"So, are you going to cut his piece, or shall I? There isn't very much left."

Lexia groaned, dug out a to-go container and filled it with a slice. She held it up for Sam's approval. "Happy?"

"Khalil will be."

"I'll be in my office." Once there, she placed the container on her desk and dropped down into her chair. Brandon had flipped the conversation and handled her with such finesse she didn't realize what happened until it was too late. "The man is probably ruthless in a boardroom," she muttered, and rotated her chair to her computer.

After two hours, Lexia leaned back and thought about how to manage the visit with Khalil. No doubt he would still be very angry and frustrated. How would he react to her visit? Would he ignore her as he'd done his family? Maybe she should tell Brandon it might be better if she waited to visit. She drummed her fingers on the desk for a moment then reached for her cell phone to send a text to Elyse. She filled her friend in on the explosion, Khalil's injury and hearing loss and asked for some advice on what to do. She set the phone aside and turned her attention to the revised menu she had been working on.

The phone chimed with a text a while later and Lexia picked it up.

Elyse: I'm so sorry to hear about Khalil. Don't approach him like you and Janice did with me.

Lexia: I don't understand.

Elyse: The 'oh, you poor thing' approach. I'm sure he has enough people doing that. Be yourself, Lexi, and talk to him the same way you did last week. He needs to know that he's still the same, in spite of what's happened.

Lexia: Thanks. :)

Elyse: Let me know how it goes.

Lexia: I will.

"Lexia, Samantha wants to know if you can come out front for a few minutes. She has to deliver a lunch order upstairs."

Lexia's head came up. "Sure, Jayla. Tell her I'll be right there." She placed her cell in the drawer, saved the changes on her file and closed it and donned her apron.

She took orders and delivered food for the next forty-five minutes until the lunch rush had passed and only a handful of customers remained. She started back to the kitchen with an armload of empty plates and stopped short upon seeing Brandon entering. "Hey, Brandon. Give me a minute."

Brandon stepped to the side so she could pass. "No problem."

Lexia placed the dishes in the dishpan and poked her head around the industrial-size refrigerator to speak to the chef. "Mr. Willis, I'll be gone for about an hour and a half. If there is something you need to add to the inventory list, just leave it on my desk if I'm not back by the time you leave."

Mr. Willis stuck his bearded face around the door. "You going to get supplies?"

"No. Visit a friend in the hospital."

He paused. "That fella you were sitting with that got hurt the other day?"

"Yes." He scrutinized her with an intensity that almost made her squirm.

He wagged a thick finger her way. "You be careful. I don't want to see you going through the same mess again."

Lexia smiled. This man had been a fixture in her life since she was a teen and was another inspiration on her journey to become a chef. She remembered him telling her, "Cooking up something that tastes good always makes you feel better." Over the years, he'd added some girth around his middle and a few lines bracketed his light brown face, but his warm smile had not changed. "Don't worry. I'll be fine." She leaned up and kissed his cheek. "See you in a bit."

She stopped by her office to get the coffee cake and her purse. As she lifted it from the drawer, she spotted Khalil's phone and picked it up. She'd totally forgotten about it. On her way out, she passed the small mirror hanging on the wall and realized she still had on the apron and hairnet.

"Good grief, girl." Lexia removed both and took a moment to fix her hair before going out to meet Brandon.

"Ready?" Brandon asked.

"Yes." She glanced over her shoulder. "I'll be back, Sam."

"Take your time. We'll close up if you're not back."

Lexia didn't see any reason why she wouldn't be back before closing. She didn't plan on staying more than a few minutes. He led her to the parking garage, stopped at a late model black Mercedes and held the door open for her. She slid into the butter-soft seat and scanned the interior. *Their family company must be doing well.*

He got in on the other side, started the engine and pulled away. For a few minutes, they rode in companionable silence. Then he asked, "How did you come to own the café?"

A smile touched her lips. "A friend of mine let me know that it was closing and knew I was looking for a place." When Cameron told Lexia about the previous owners going under, he had almost begged her to lease the space. He'd mentioned the food being terrible and the tenants in the building wanting the convenience of an in-house place for food. Lexia had been still reeling from her divorce and the loss of her first diner and wasn't sure she wanted to go through the hassle again. But Cameron and Janice, along with Samantha, had helped Lexia with the down payment and it had turned out to be the best thing she had done.

"Well, on behalf of everyone in the building, thank you. I hate to say it, but before you took over, the only thing I went there for was coffee. The food was terrible."

She laughed. "Yeah, I heard that and I'm glad you're enjoying the food. Khalil mentioned that you have a family-owned company. What do you do there?"

Brandon slanted her a quick glance, then refocused on the road. "I took over as CEO last year."

"Oh. Wow." She didn't know what she expected—a management position for sure—but CEO? "Do you have any other siblings?"

"Two sisters and another brother. Only my older sister and I work for the company, though. What about you?"

"No. My parents wanted more than one, but after two miscarriages, stopped trying. Between music and all my extracurricular activities, my mother always said I kept her busy enough for three children."

He chuckled. "Multiply that times five and you have our family."

Lexia shook her head. "I can't even imagine. It must have been great to always have a playmate." Being an only child had been lonely at times and she often wished she had a sister to share secrets with. Elyse and Janice had filled that role somewhat.

"It had its moments." For the remainder of the drive, Brandon shared stories of his and his siblings' antics.

When they got to the hospital entrance, a case of nerves hit her. They took the elevator to Khalil's floor and she followed Brandon's long strides down the hallway. She could hear Khalil two doors down and he did not sound happy.

"Here we go again," Brandon muttered. "My sister, Siobhan, must be trying to get him to eat again."

Lexia heard Khalil yell, "Vonnie, I said let it go!"

When they reached the door, Brandon gestured Lexia forward. "Go ahead. Maybe he won't take your head off."

Although he'd made the remark teasingly, his grim expression told all. "It's going to take him some time to adjust."

"I know. He's the most easygoing of us all and it's just hard seeing him like this."

She felt for him, for their family. Steeling herself, she pushed the door open.

Khalil stopped midsentence. "Lexia?"

She gave him a tiny wave and walked fully into the room. A tall, curvy woman dressed to the nines in a gold suit that fit her like a glove turned and stared. She bore a strong resemblance to Brandon and Khalil, including eye color, except hers were a shade lighter, almost golden.

Brandon made the introductions. "Lexia, this is my sister, Siobhan. Vonnie, this is Lexia. She's the one who was with Khalil when he got hurt and the owner of Oasis Café."

"It's nice to meet you, Siobhan," Lexia said.

Siobhan smiled. "Same here. Thanks for being there with my brother, and bless you for taking over the café."

Lexia returned her smile. "You're welcome." Siobhan handed her a cell.

"You can talk to him through here and he can read it on his."

Because of Elyse, she already knew about the app, but nodded. She approached the bed and hoped she wasn't next in line to have her head taken off.

Lexia stood to the left of the bed. "I'm glad to see you're feeling better. I was worried about you."

Khalil tried his best to sound cheerful. "Thanks. I'm fine."

"I brought you something." She placed a container on the bed tray and opened it.

The coffee cake. As much as he enjoyed it, right now the only thing he wanted was his hearing. "You didn't need to bring that and I can't eat."

She frowned. "Are you on a special diet?"

"No."

"Then you can eat it." She rolled the tray in front of him and produced a fork.

He stared at her a long moment. "Lexia, I know you—" She lifted his left hand, moved it around, turned it over and wiggled his fingers. He snatched his hand back. "What are you doing?" Ignoring him, she leaned closer, cupped his

jaw in her hand and ran her finger across his lips. Khalil
brushed her hand aside. "What are you doing?"

"You said you couldn't eat and I was trying to find out
why. Your hand moves just fine and, with all the fussing
you're doing, there's nothing wrong with your mouth, either. So, what's your problem?"

Khalil read the words on the screen in disbelief. He met
her challenging stare.

Lexia handed him the fork and gestured to the coffee
cake. "Eat."

He didn't need to read the screen to know what she'd
said. Siobhan stared at Lexia in shock and Brandon outright laughed. He didn't need to hear to know that, either.
He grudgingly took the fork, cut a piece of the cake and
stuck it in his mouth. "Happy?"

She smiled and pointed toward the door. "I'll be right
back."

He nodded. As soon as the door closed, he shot a lethal
glare at his brother. "Shut up, Brandon."

Lexia was back in a flash holding a cup with a tea bag
hanging from the side. "Decaf vanilla chai with one raw
sugar and a dash of milk." She peeked into the container
and frowned.

"I know, I know. I'm eating."

She smiled. "Hey, I'm just trying to finish that date you
owe me. We got interrupted."

Khalil shook his head and couldn't stop the smile that
crept out. "Hell, for all this badgering, you owe me a *real*
date."

Her eyes widened for a split second. "Okay."

Their eyes held for a moment longer, then he resumed
eating. Brandon and Siobhan slipped out the door, leaving
Khalil and Lexia alone.

She reached into her purse and handed him his cell phone. "I found it after you were gone."

"Thanks." He had totally forgotten about the phone and was glad she'd found it, rather than someone else. Otherwise, it would be one more thing added to the list of things to do. He turned the power on and checked it out. Aside from a cracked screen, the phone still worked fine.

She held her hand out. "I'll leave you my number just in case you need anything...or want to chat."

He'd wanted her phone number—had planned to ask for it the day of the explosion—but couldn't see her or any other woman being willing to go out with a man who was... He refused to say the word. Instead, he opened the new contact page and handed it to her. She input her information and passed it back.

When he finished eating, Lexia threw the empty container away. His gaze followed her and he still could not believe her ordering him around. Everybody else had approached him with pity, but not Lexia. And what was he thinking asking her on a date? He couldn't take her out—not now. He wouldn't be able to communicate with the waitstaff or her without these stupid phones. He didn't even know if he could drive. And having her pick him up was out of the question.

Lexia came back and sat next to him. "What did the doctor say?"

Khalil repeated what Dr. Moyer had told him. "So I don't know when my hearing will come back...which is why I don't think we should have that date right now."

She angled her head thoughtfully. "What does that have to do with anything? Lots of deaf people go out to eat."

His jaw tightened. *Deaf.* Why did she have to call it that? He wasn't deaf. He just had a temporary hearing loss. He pushed the tray aside and carefully shifted in the bed. "I'm a little tired. Thanks for bringing me the coffee cake." He didn't miss the flash of sadness in her eyes. "We can talk about the date thing once I get out of here and settled at home," he added, trying to soften his abrupt manner.

Lexia stood. "That's fine. I'm glad you're feeling better. Do you need anything before I go?"

"No."

"Then I'll see you later." She gave his hand a squeeze, hesitated, then leaned down to kiss his cheek.

Khalil impulsively shifted and turned what she meant as a friendly peck into something hot and all consuming. He slid his hand into the mass of curls and held her in place. He remembered the warmth of her lips when she had brushed them against his while lying on the sidewalk. There had been something about her touch and her kiss that did something to him. It was calming and…he didn't know what, but wanted to feel that sensation again. Needed it at this moment.

At length, Lexia lifted her head. Without another word, she walked out.

Khalil blew out a long breath. His hearing had to come back soon because he didn't know how much longer he could take this.

Chapter 6

After being cooped up in the hospital for four days, Khalil was glad to get home Saturday afternoon. Well, he would be as soon as his family left. His mother had insisted on being there when he arrived and, although he tried to tell her he could manage on his own, she had cooked enough food to last him for at least a week. Yes, his ribs were still sore—the doctor said they should heal in a few weeks—but he could maneuver around his kitchen. Leaving her in the kitchen, he slowly walked up the stairs leading to his bedroom for some peace, but found his sisters changing the sheets on his bed. Khalil appreciated their enthusiasm, but he just wanted to take some pain medication and lie down.

Both women looked up when he entered the room and rushed toward him. They each took an arm. "Vonnie and Morgan, I can walk by myself." He gently disentangled himself and made his way to one of the plush chairs positioned in front of the fireplace.

"I love you, but can you please hurry up with my bed, so I can get in it?"

"We'll be done in a moment."

"This pain—" He groaned inwardly. That was the absolute wrong thing to say because Siobhan dropped the edge of the sheet in her hand and rushed over to where he sat.

Siobhan's concerned gaze roamed over his face as she mouthed with exaggerated movement, "Are you in pain? Where's your medication?"

Khalil grabbed one of her hands and placed a kiss on the back. "Relax, sis. I'll be fine after I lie down for a while." As soon as the words left his mouth, Morgan materialized at his side with two pills and glass of water. "Thanks, Morgan." He swallowed them with a few sips of the cool liquid

and handed the glass back. A few minutes later, they finished making the bed. "I appreciate you making the bed.
Now go home to your husbands and to my niece. I'm sure
Nyla is looking for her mama," he said to Siobhan. She had
given birth to the little girl seven months ago and he loved
his role as uncle. The thought of never hearing her sweet
laughter again sent a sharp pain through his chest.

He kissed both women and shooed them out. He let out
a sigh of relief and he climbed in, glad to finally be in his
own bed again. A heartbeat later, he was asleep.

When Khalil woke up two hours later, he felt much better. He sat up and swung his legs over the side of the bed
and sat for a minute to get his bearings. In the hospital,
he'd had to make do with sponge baths, so a hot shower
topped his priority list. He left his room and peered over
the rail and into the living room. It was blessedly empty.
He retraced his steps to the bedroom, stripped and headed
for the bathroom.

The pain and weakness in his sprained wrist proved to
be a slight challenge, but he managed to wash up and dry
off. He really needed a shave and haircut, but he didn't
have the energy to do that right now. He cinched the towel
around his waist, stepped back into the bedroom and froze.

His mother's eyes widened, he saw her mouth move and
she spun around.

Khalil groaned, grabbed a robe from the closet and put
it on. "Mom, what are you doing here? I thought you were
gone."

Without turning around, she held up the cell phone, then
spoke into it.

He picked up the other one from the nightstand, left, of
course, by one of his sisters and read: "Are you decent?"

"Yes, Mom."

His mother took a quick peek over her shoulder, and then

turned around. She folded her arms and frowned. "You shouldn't be walking around half-naked."

He lifted a brow. "I live alone, Mom, so it's usually not a problem. Anyway, you didn't answer my question. What are you doing here?"

"You need someone to look after you."

A vision of what that might entail flashed in his mind and a wave of dread washed over him.

She continued. "What if the phone rings or you need to call someone?"

"It's the twenty-first century. There's email, texting… I'll figure something out. I thought you and Dad were supposed to be leaving for a cruise in a couple of weeks. I'm sure you have lots of shopping and packing to do, and Dad is probably wondering where his dinner is. I'm fine on my own and if I need something, I'll figure it out. If I can't, I promise to let someone know." Khalil crossed the room, placed his arm around her shoulder and steered her out of the room, down the stairs and toward the front door, stopping to pick up her purse from the sofa.

She focused her determined mama expression on him—the one that said she would fight him tooth and nail to get her way. "In case you've forgotten, young man, I'm the mother. Your father is perfectly capable of heating leftovers and I don't need two weeks to pack. You are not fine on your own. You—"

"Yes, Mama, I *am* fine on my own. I'll admit that there are a few things I have to learn to do, and I'm sure all of that will be taken care of on my follow-up appointment with the specialist. In the meantime, I'll deal."

Tears welled in her eyes and her lip quivered.

Please don't let her start crying again. She'd done enough of that at the hospital. He released a deep sigh. He was tempted to just let her stay if only to keep her from crying, but the last time she'd camped out at one of their homes, she had rearranged all the furniture and reorganized the kitchen. Malcolm had complained for weeks about not being able to find anything and had to go through the process of changing his furniture back. Khalil liked his place and had everything where he wanted. And he enjoyed the freedom of being able to walk around butt naked if he wanted without an audience.

"You're stubborn just like your father," she said.

He wanted to tell her he had gotten it honestly, but said, "I'll take that as a compliment." He took in her attire. She had on a pair of navy sweats and matching sweatshirt. Most people would have on tennis shoes, but not his mother. Her idea of dressing down included a pair of loafers and a scarf around her neck. As always, she wore light makeup and not one strand of her layered salt-and-pepper cropped hair was out of place.

Glaring at him, she snatched her purse from his outstretched hand, slung it over her shoulder and slapped the cell down on his palm.

He placed a kiss on her temple. "I love you, Mom. I'll send you a text in a couple of hours to let you know I'm okay. How's that?"

She nodded, stroked a loving hand down his cheek and walked out.

Khalil stood there for a moment before going to get dressed. Contrary to what he'd told his mother, he wasn't fine. He had no clue how to deal with this. He opened the sliding glass door and stepped out onto the balcony in his bedroom. The late March temperatures hovered in the sixties and a crisp breeze blew across his face. He could see the birds circling above, people jogging down the beach and the waves crashing against the shore. He strained his ears, searching for some kind of sound. Nothing. Usually, the sounds of the ocean and waves filled him with a sense of peace, but today he felt lost. How did people live this way? How was *he* going to live this way? And for how long? Khalil went back inside, locked the door and headed to the kitchen. After fifteen minutes of searching, he decided on a smoothie. He still had no appetite and hadn't eaten much outside of the coffee cake Lexia had brought two days ago. Her visit had been a total surprise. Had she wanted to come or had Brandon somehow coerced her? He didn't see her being easily swayed by anyone. It had even taken him some doing just to convince her to sit with him at her own café, humbling for a man who'd never in his life had a problem getting a woman. He had promised her a date, but refused to do it until everything was back to normal. A part of him worried that she might have moved on by then, but a bigger part of him couldn't bring himself to get involved with a woman while he was like *this*.

Monday morning, Lexia loaded the supplies from her car onto a cart and entered the café through the back door.

"Why didn't you tell me you had all this stuff?" Mr. Willis fussed as he rushed over to take the cart.

"It's no big deal. I do it all the time." She rubbed her hands together to warm them. It was barely five in the morning and the March winds were living up to their name.

"Not when I'm here. I thought we cleared that up a long time ago."

She smiled. "I know, but you were busy with the pastries and I didn't want to interrupt your flow."

Mr. Willis stopped near the refrigerator and unloaded the items that needed to stay cold. "Five minutes ain't gonna hurt nothing. I'll take care of this." He gestured toward the counters. "You go on and get started with that coffee cake."

"Yes, sir!" She gave the former army drill sergeant a

crisp salute, turned on her heel and marched over to the counter.

His deep laughter filled the kitchen. "You should've joined the army. Your salute is better than half the clowns in my platoon."

Still smiling, Lexia got to work. By the time she put the cake into the oven, the fragrant smells of all the food made her stomach growl. She had gone shopping the night before and stopped at a twenty-four-hour grocery store on her way in this morning to pick up the few items not available at the local Costco. As a result, she'd skipped having her typical breakfast of fruit and chamomile tea.

When Sam arrived an hour later, at six, Lexia was on her way to her office to eat an English muffin and drink her tea. "Morning, Sam."

"Morning, girl," Sam said around a yawn.

She took a sip of her tea. "Late night?"

A sly smile curved Sam's lips. "You could say that. Aaron was especially—"

Lexia held up a hand. "Just stop. I don't need to hear the details. That's just TMI."

Sam lifted a brow. "You could be having your own late nights with that fine Khalil Gray if you weren't so stubborn."

"Whatever." She rolled her eyes and bit into the English muffin.

"Speaking of Khalil, how is he doing?"

"I haven't spoken to him or Brandon since my visit on Thursday, so I don't know. Brandon did mention something about Khalil probably going home sometime over the weekend." She had given him her number, but he had yet to text her and she tried not to let it bother her. She also didn't want to keep asking Brandon for updates and was too chicken to ask him for Khalil's number.

"Well, you said that he's having a hard time accepting his condition, so I'm not surprised. He probably thinks he's damaged goods and no woman would want him."

"But he's not," Lexia said, sitting at her desk.

Sam folded her arms and leaned against the door frame. "I know that and you know that, but it'll take him some time to figure it out. You know as well as I do that men have a lot of pride."

"And he has some asinine belief that this will somehow make him less of a man." She recalled him telling her they should wait to go out. At first, she had felt a twinge of disappointment, but later realized he was afraid. And she clearly saw his frustration with having to use the speech-to-text app.

"You got it, sis." Sam straightened. "I assume the coffee cake is out of the oven."

She nodded and finished chewing. "I'll cut it when I'm done eating."

She waved Lexia off. "I'll do it. Finish your food."

"Thanks. I'll be out by the time we open."

"Okay. I'm going to see if Mr. Willis can make me one of his omelets. I tried to make one over the weekend and ended up throwing half the thing out. I don't know how he gets his to taste so good."

"Easy. He's been making them longer than we've been alive, as he always tells me."

Sam chuckled. "Whatever the reason, I need one to make up for my pitiful attempt."

Lexia laughed and went back to her food.

Later, she and Sam handled the morning rush and Lexia stayed out front until Jayla came in at ten and she could retreat to her office.

An hour later, the college student poked her head in the office. "Lexia, there's a woman out here asking for you."

"Is it Elyse?"

"Nope. I think she works in the building. I've seen her in the café several times for lunch. She's tall, has kind of golden-brown eyes…"

Siobhan? Brandon mentioned one of his sisters working for their company. Lexia swiftly came to her feet. Had something happened to Khalil?

"Oh, and the guy she's with is to die for. There are some fine men working in this building. I may have to change my major."

Chuckling, she followed Jayla and saw Siobhan sitting across the table from a clean-shaven mahogany-skinned man who was every bit as fine as Jayla said.

"Told you," Jayla said with a smile, following Lexia's gaze.

Lexia approached the couple and the man started to rise. "Please don't get up."

Siobhan gestured. "Lexia, this is my husband, Justin."

"Nice to meet you, Justin."

"Same here."

She focused her attention on Siobhan. "Did something happen to Khalil? Is he okay?"

"Depends on your definition of *okay*. Physically, he's healing well. Emotionally, I don't think so and we don't have a clue what to do. He doesn't want us to help and he's pretty much stopped answering all of our texts."

"Is he still in the hospital?"

"No, he came home on Saturday. My sister and I offered to take turns staying with him, but he refused. And my mother said he all but put her out yesterday."

"I'm sorry to hear that. This has to be really hard for him."

"It is and I'm hoping you can help."

"Me? Um…I don't know how I can help you. I'm sure the specialist can give you some resources."

Siobhan nodded. "True. I'm sure he will when Khalil goes for his appointment tomorrow. But my brother responded to you differently than he has anyone else. He didn't yell at you or throw you out of his room. *And* you're the only one who's been able to get him to crack a smile in a week. So yeah, I think you're just the person he needs." She smiled. "I also heard that Khalil likes you, and that's a plus in my book. If you stop by his place, I guarantee he'll let you in."

Lexia felt her eyes widen. *"His place?"* Visiting Khalil in the hospital was one thing, but going to his home? "I don't think that's a good idea. Maybe after he's…" She trailed off, not knowing what to say.

"You're good." She held up her cell phone. "I just texted him and told him you asked if it would be okay if you visited and he answered *yes*."

Justin chuckled. "You'll have to forgive my wife. She's the PR director and, as you can tell, she's very good at manipulating things to her advantage."

"That's an understatement," Lexia mumbled.

"Hey, I have to use what I can to help my brother. Khalil has always been the voice of reason and the most even-tempered of all of us. Now he's angry and hurting and he won't let us help," Siobhan added, her voice cracking.

Justin reached for his wife's hand. "Baby, I told you, Khalil needs some time to adjust. And I'm sure this is temporary. He'll get his hearing back soon."

Lexia hoped he was right. She and Janice had tried reassuring Elyse that hers would return, too. But it never happened. After hearing Khalil's outburst at the hospital and the way he refused to consider going out, she imagined the longer his recovery took, the further he would retreat. As much as she wanted to help him, she didn't want to get her feelings hurt. However, the plea in Siobhan's eyes made it hard to say no. "Maybe I should wait until after his doctor's appointment to see how he feels before planning a visit."

"I hope it's soon."

"We'll see. I'll let you two get back to your lunch. It was nice to meet you, Justin."

"Nice meeting you, too, Lexia."

She hightailed it back to her office. While she understood Siobhan's urgency and was, admittedly, curious about him and where he lived, Lexia had no intention of going to Khalil's home unless he invited her. And she didn't see that happening anytime soon.

Her cell buzzed, letting her know she had a text message. She didn't recognize the number and figured it was one of those telemarketers. She had no idea how these people kept getting her information. Her finger hovered over the delete button for a second, then she decided to read it:

My sister said you wanted to visit. You can come tomorrow after you get off work. Here's my address. The building has valet parking and you can text me when you get to my door.

Khalil. She'd thought for sure he wouldn't contact her. Wrong. She scrolled down to his address. Marina del Rey? So, not only did he work near where she lived, but they were also practically neighbors.

Lexia: How are you?

Khalil: I'm fine.

Lexia: Are you sure you're up to a visit? I'll understand if you aren't.

Khalil: I'm sure.

Lexia: Is there anything you'd like me to bring you, something you need?

Khalil: No. But thanks. I'll see you tomorrow.

Lexia took that to mean the conversation was over. She tossed the cell on her desk. *Guess I'll be making that visit after all.*

Chapter 7

Khalil's frustration mounted as he sat reading what Dr. Moyer was saying. The man could have said all this at the hospital, instead of wasting his time today. There had been no change in the holes in his eardrums and the doctor cautioned Khalil again to keep them dry.

"What about driving?"

The doctor picked up a stack of brochures and papers from the counter. "There's no reason you can't drive, no laws prohibiting it. You'll just have to rely on your sense of sight a little more." He passed the stack to Khalil. "Here are some resources for you. There's a brochure on technology for your telephone, doorbell, alarm clocks and things like that. I also included some information on sign language."

"Sign language? Why would I learn sign language if my hearing is going to return?" He didn't see the need to spend time mastering something that he wouldn't need past a month or two.

"We have no idea how much of your hearing will return... or if it will at all. I'd rather you be prepared just in case."

Khalil clenched his jaw and tightened his grip on the communication cell. He resisted the urge to throw it and the brochures across the room. "Is there anything else?"

Dr. Moyer went to the computer. "No. I'd like to see you in four weeks or sooner if you start to hear any sounds." He typed something, checked a few boxes and logged off. "You can schedule with the receptionist."

"Fine." He stood and preceded the doctor out of the door. After scheduling his next appointment, he went back out to the waiting room, where Malcolm sat.

Malcolm jumped to his feet. "What did he say?"

Khalil shook his head and pointed toward the door.

Though there were only three people seated, he didn't want his business spread across the waiting room. As soon as they got into the car, his phone buzzed with a text from Malcolm repeating the question he'd asked. Unlike the rest of his family, Malcolm preferred texting to using the speech app.

"There's no change. He just gave me a bunch of brochures on stuff to use around the house. And information on sign language classes." Just saying the words made him cringe. Agreeing to take those classes was akin to accepting his condition. And he wasn't.

Sounds like a good plan.

"It's not. I don't need to waste my time on something that's temporary."

Malcolm stared at him.

"Can we leave now?" Instead of starting the car, his brother sent another text. Khalil groaned inwardly, but read it. Thankfully, Malcolm had let the subject drop, but asked if Khalil wanted to stop by the gym. "Not today. I'll go over in a couple of days." He'd had enough of the pitiful looks people gave him.

Alonzo has the information from the cameras and your computer. He said the accounts haven't been touched and to contact him. He placed his cell in a cup holder, started the car and pulled out of the lot.

"Good." Khalil leaned his head back and closed his eyes. As long as there hadn't been any more charges, he could deal with the rest later.

When they pulled up to Khalil's place, Malcolm picked up his cell. Do you want me to come up?

"No. When are you leaving for the Caribbean?" Every

year, Malcolm took a month-long trip before the start of football season.

His hand paused over the screen. I haven't decided.

Khalil studied Malcolm. Four years Khalil's junior, the twenty-nine-year-old star running back never missed his vacation. "I know you aren't hesitating because of me."

He nodded.

"Go on your vacation, Malcolm. I'm sure Mom, Siobhan or Morgan will keep you updated." Khalil reached for the door handle.

Malcolm laid a hand on Khalil's arm. Do you need me to drive you over to the gym when you go?

"No. I can drive myself." He didn't know how that would work, but he had to figure it out. He got out of the car, threw up a wave and headed into the lobby. Just like when he came home on Saturday, it unnerved him to see everyone's mouths moving and not be able to hear the buzz of conversation around him or the footsteps behind him. All the sounds he had taken for granted were now gone and the world seemed like it was closing in on him. He quickened his steps to the elevator and jabbed the button. The doors opened and he stepped inside. Khalil took a deep breath and instantly regretted it. A sharp pain reminded him that his ribs were still healing. What the hell was happening to him? His chest tightened and his hands shook. Thankfully, he rode to his floor without anyone else getting on. He felt as if someone had dropped him into a soundproof room with no way out. The silence closed in on him and he thought he would explode.

Inside his condo, Khalil tossed his keys on an end table and lowered himself to the sofa. He stretched out and drew in a calming breath, this time being careful not to inhale too deeply. He lay there staring at the vaulted ceiling until the rumbling of his stomach forced him to the kitchen for food.

He grabbed an apple from the fruit bowl on the counter and a napkin and went to sit outside on the balcony.

Khalil thought about all the information Dr. Moyer had given him. He would probably have to do something about the phone and doorbell soon. Otherwise, his mother would definitely move in. Thinking about her reminded him that he needed to update her on his doctor's visit. He took a bite of the apple, set it on the napkin and pulled out his phone. He made sure to give her all the details up front and tried to anticipate all her questions.

She responded almost immediately: You must have known I was about to text you. Thank you for the information.

She seemed satisfied with the response and hopefully, that meant she wouldn't be on her way over. He polished off the apple, wrapped the core in the napkin and placed it on the small table. A wave of fatigue washed over him and he leaned back in the lounger. He rarely got sick and being laid low like this irritated him. Just the short trip to the doctor's office had worn him out. Khalil glanced at his watch. He still had a couple of hours before Lexia arrived. He considered canceling, but the memory of her kiss stopped him. He just wished he could hear her voice again.

Tuesday afternoon, Lexia went to lock the door and stopped short upon seeing Cameron. She held the door open. "Come on in."

"I know you're locking up, so I won't keep you."

"You're fine. You want me to fix you something to eat?" She had plenty of time to get to Khalil's house.

Cameron nodded. "Please."

She waved him into a booth. "Have a seat. What would you like?"

"I don't want you to go to any trouble. Just bring me whatever you have left over."

Lexia placed a hand on her hip. "You know me better than that, Cameron Hughes." She retrieved a menu and slapped it down on the table. "Now, again, what would you like?"

He scratched his head and took the menu. "The bacon cheeseburger, fries and a chocolate milk shake."

"That's better." She tossed him a wink and went to the kitchen. "I'm going to fix Cameron a burger," she told her chef. "You can go ahead and leave."

Mr. Willis slanted her a glance. "You just march your little self away from my stove. I'll take care of it. He wants fries, too?"

"Yes, sir." He gave her another look. She smiled and went to make the shake. She carried it over to the table and slid in across from Cam. "I got tossed out of the kitchen."

Cameron chuckled. "He's even bossier than you."

Her mouth fell open. "*Bossy?* I am not bossy."

He put the straw in the glass, took a long sip, and then leaned back. "Lexia, you are the bossiest woman I know... next to my Jan. The two of you together were always trouble. It's a good thing Elyse was there to balance everything out."

Lexia had to laugh. Growing up, she and Janice had no problems setting someone straight. "Well, what can I say? People always thought they could walk all over me because I'm short. I couldn't let them get away with that." She shrugged. "So, is everything okay?" Though she was glad to see him, Cam never came around two weeks in a row.

"I was thinking more about what we talked about last week." He released a deep sigh. "I'm tired, Lexi. Tired of wandering, tired of sleeping in the cold and heat...just tired."

"Then stay here."

"I'll pay you back as soon as I find a job. In the meantime, I'll clean up around here."

"Cam, you don't need to pay me anything. You do remember that you and Jan fronted me money for this place."

"Which you paid back two months later."

"I'm not taking any money from you, so forget it. The room is yours until you get back on your feet. And if you need an address for job applications, use mine."

"Thanks, Lexia."

Mr. Willis brought the food over and observed Cameron. "You ready to come in from the cold, young man?"

"Yes, sir."

He clapped Cam on the shoulder and nodded. "Let me know if I can help."

"Thank you," Cam whispered.

Lexia's heart swelled. After Mr. Willis walked away, she told Cam, "You could probably get your old job back." He had worked in finance at one of the companies located on the third floor of the building.

Cam shook his head as he bit into the burger. He chewed and swallowed before speaking. "Too many memories. I want to start fresh."

"I can understand that."

Samantha came in from the back. "Hey, Lexi. What are you still doing here? I thought you were going over to Khalil's. Oh, hey, Cam."

"Hey, Samantha." Cam fixed his gaze on Lexia. "Who's Khalil? Wait. Is that the guy who got hurt last week? The one who looked like he wanted to break me in half."

Lexia's face heated. "I don't know about the whole 'break you in half' thing, but yeah, that's him."

"Well, you'd better get going. I can just take this to go."

"Go? Didn't you just tell me you were going to stay here?" She hopped up from the booth.

"I'll come back tomorrow. That way you'll have time to—"

She held up a hand. "I don't need time to fix anything up. It's already done. I had a key made for you months ago in hopes that you would take me up on the offer. There are sheets, blankets, towels, soap…all the essentials for tonight. We can get whatever else you need tomorrow. I'll be right back." She went to her office and came back with a key and a card. This is the key to the back door and here's the alarm code. I'll show you where it is."

"Sam can show me. You have somewhere to be."

"He's right," Sam said. "And I'll lock up."

Lexia divided her gaze between the two. "Okay. I'll see you tomorrow. And, Cam, I'm glad you're here."

"Me, too. Oh, and tell Khalil if he breaks your heart, I'm going to break *him*."

She rolled her eyes. "It's not like that. I'm just making sure he's okay." At least that's what she told herself.

Cam folded his arms. "Whatever you say. But I meant what I said."

Sam merely smiled.

"Bye, you two."

In the parking lot, Lexia plugged Khalil's address into her GPS and pulled away. Of course, there was traffic. The normal thirty-minute drive took fifty minutes.

She could only stare when she drove up to the expensive high-rise condominium property. She picked up the bag on her seat, climbed out and turned her car over to the valet, who directed her to the security desk in the lobby. "Hello. My name is Lexia Daniels and I'm here to see Khalil Gray."

The man checked a list, found her name and nodded. He rose, escorted her over to the elevators and stuck a key into the penthouse slot. "Enjoy your visit." He stepped out and doors closed.

Lexia was even more curious. The doors opened and she walked down the plush carpeted hallway. There were only three condos on the floor. Several beach landscapes lined the walls. She went the wrong way and had to double back. His was at the other end of the hall. Taking a deep breath, she sent him a text. Moments later, the door opened. She gave him a tiny wave.

"Hey." He stepped back and gestured her in.

Magnificent. That was the only word that came to mind as she entered. The wood floors gleamed in the sunlight that streamed in from two walls of windows in the living room. The wide-open space flowed into a kitchen twice the size of hers with granite counters, stainless steel appliances, maple cabinets and access to a large terrace that held four loungers and a couple of small bistro tables. She walked over to one of the windows. He had a stunning view of the marina and ocean. She faced him and spoke slowly. "I like this."

"Thanks." Khalil walked over to an end table next to a black leather sofa, retrieved the same phone she'd used at the hospital and handed it to her. "Do you want to see the rest of the place?"

"I'd love to. And I can just download the chat app on my phone, so it'll be easier." She took a moment to do that and synced it to his phone. Now she really wanted to see his place and was glad he had offered. She followed him down the hall past a bathroom with a shower and a carpeted bedroom decorated in shades of tans and browns. Next they climbed the winding staircase to the second floor to his huge master bedroom with another fabulous view of the water. A king-size bed covered with a black-and-gray comforter sat on one side of the room, while a fireplace surrounded by two oversize recliners and a wooden coffee table took up the other side. A flat-screen television was mounted on the wall opposite the bed.

Lexia walked farther into the room and saw an expansive walk-in closet that looked custom-built. Everything was neatly in its place and she wondered if he had someone who came in to clean. Next she headed for the en suite bathroom. He had a whirlpool tub and separate shower with smoke-gray glass. Both were large enough to fit two people easily. "This is a fabulous place. How long have you lived here?"

"Six years. I needed a permanent place to live after I stopped modeling and I wanted to be close to the beach. I lucked up on this place when it foreclosed on the previous owners."

She surveyed the room again. Even if he had purchased it at a foreclosed price, it still wasn't cheap. Obviously, he'd done well with his modeling career. Lexia recalled the photos she had seen. Yeah, he'd done *real* well.

"I was going to heat up some homemade chicken noodle soup my sister left. Would you like to join me?"

"Sure." She followed him back downstairs. She sensed his uncertainty and wanted to tell him it was okay. Unlike their first times together, he didn't flirt, and gone was the playful glint in his eyes. She sat at the table in the eat-in area and watched as he moved around the kitchen.

"What do you want to drink? I have water, green tea and cranberry juice."

"I'll take the tea, please."

Khalil leaned over the bar to read the screen then nodded. He filled two glasses with tea, brought them to the table and went back for the bowls of soup and the phone.

They ate in silence for a few minutes. She touched his hand softly to get his attention. He still wore the brace for his sprained wrist. "This is really good. Which sister cooked it? Siobhan?"

"Yes, and I'll be sure to tell her."

"How are you doing with everything?"

His jaw tightened, but he didn't answer.

"You don't have to answer. I understand."

He gave a sarcastic chuckle. "You understand? Do you understand how it feels to have everyone look at you with pity and think you can't do the things you used to do? Do you know how it feels to have your ears ringing so loud you think your head is going to explode? Do you understand how it feels to not be able to hear your own voice, the radio or the waves crashing against the shore? *Do you?*"

Lexia bit her lip and tried to keep the tears from falling. She knew he was lashing out because he was frustrated, but it hurt all the same. She swiftly came to her feet. "I think I should go." Rushing from the table, she made her way to the living room, where she'd left her purse.

"Lexia, don't go." Khalil gently took hold of her hand and pulled her into his arms. "Please don't leave. I'm sorry." He leaned back and tilted her chin to meet his tormented gaze. "I didn't mean to... Please don't cry." He framed her face with his hands and wiped away her tears with the pads of his thumbs. "I'm sorry, baby. So sorry."

He lowered his head and covered her mouth in a tender kiss that she felt clear to her toes. She wrapped her arms around his middle, pressed closer to his hard body and let herself be swept away in the sweet sensations.

"Stay with me."

She hesitated briefly, then nodded.

Khalil took her hand and led her back to the table, where they finished their meal.

Lexia didn't offer any conversation. She was still trying to process the emotional surge from his kiss. Yes, she was attracted to him, but she didn't need any upheaval in her life right now. She lifted her head and found him staring at her intently. He covered her hand with his briefly, then picked up his spoon.

Afterward, they went back upstairs to his bedroom, where he got a blanket from a chest. "Come sit with me for a while." He gingerly lowered himself to the cushioned lounger on his balcony, positioned her between his legs and covered her with the blanket. "Are you warm enough?"

Lexia nodded. He wrapped his arms around her and she snuggled deeper into his embrace, being careful not to put her weight on his injured ribs. Together, they sat and watched the sunset over the ocean. She could get used to being with him this way. So not good.

Chapter 8

Khalil sat quietly holding Lexia. He couldn't believe he had yelled at her, something totally out of character for him. His only excuse—this not being able to hear a thing was making him crazy. He glanced down at her peaceful expression and wished he could experience the same. However, something told him he wouldn't be at peace until he woke up from this nightmare or learned to accept it. At this moment, the nightmare had the upper hand.

Lexia shifted.

He moved the mass of curls. "Are you cold?"

She rotated so he could see her face fully. "No."

They continued to watch the sunset. He remembered her carrying a bag in when she arrived and had planned to ask about it before he lost his mind. "What was in that bag you brought?"

She stared up at him, then pulled out her phone to type. She held it up. "Just something I thought you could use, but I'll save it for another time."

His brows knit in confusion. "Why would you want to wait if it's already here?"

She hesitated, then typed again. "After what happened earlier, I think it might be better to wait. I'd rather not have my head chopped off twice in one hour." She flashed him a meaningful look.

Khalil closed his eyes briefly. "If I promise not to chop your head off, will you show me?" He peered over her shoulder to see the screen. "Only if I can get it in writing." For the first time in a week, he laughed. Then groaned.

Lexia sat up and shook her head. She gently ran her hand down his chest. "Are you okay?"

Just like the first time she touched him, warmth flowed

through his blood. "Yeah, baby. I'm okay and I'll put whatever you want in writing." Though she didn't weigh much, with his sprained wrist and broken ribs, there would be no way he'd be able to carry her like he wanted. He placed a kiss on her temple. "Let's go see what you've got." He waited until she stood before carefully shifting and following suit.

Once downstairs, she retrieved the large green gift bag from the love seat and handed it to him. She gave him a look that said, "You promised."

He opened it, pulled out a hardback book and read the title: *The Joy of Signing*. He bit back a curse and it took everything in him not to toss the book in the fireplace and light it. He'd made a promise.

She folded her arms, waiting. A smile played around the corners of her mouth. She held up her phone.

"Having a little trouble with that promise? I don't mean to upset you, but how do you propose to communicate effectively over time if, for some reason, it takes much longer for your hearing to return? Technology is great, but what if it fails?"

Khalil lowered himself to the love seat and tossed the book and bag on the coffee table. She'd mirrored what the doctor had said. If he didn't know better, he would swear she'd been hiding in the examination room. Why had this happened to him? And why now? He had too much on his plate to have to deal with this.

Lexia sat next to him.

"I can't begin to imagine how hard this is for you, how angry you must be, but I will help you in any way I can. If you don't want to start learning sign language right now, it's fine. But you'd better not toss my book in the fireplace."

His head came up. "How did you know I was thinking that?"

"I saw your expression."

Khalil reached for the book. "This is yours?"

She nodded.

"Why would you need it?"

She signed as she talked. "To talk to my friend."

He quickly read what she said and his eyebrows shot up. "You know sign language?"

She nodded and signed.

"That's the sign for yes?" She nodded again and he sat stunned. This woman was full of surprises. She owned her own business, knew sign language. What was next? Still, he just wasn't ready to jump in, confident that he'd be hearing again in a couple of weeks. But he didn't want to hurt her feelings, so he told her, "I'll think about it."

Lexia smiled.

"Well, I should get going. You need to rest and I have some things to get done tonight. Hopefully, since it's almost eight, it won't take long for me to get home."

He should have sent her home earlier so she wouldn't have to drive at night. "I'm sorry for keeping you out so late." Normally, he would insist on following her home, but the thought of driving made him uncomfortable. *Afraid* would be a more accurate description if he were being honest with himself.

Lexia waved him off. "I'm fine. This isn't the first time I've been out at night by myself."

Maybe not. But it was a first on his watch and he didn't like it one bit.

"Anytime you want to talk…"

"Thanks."

She slung her purse on her shoulder and headed for the front door. She turned back and waved.

Instead of waving back, he lowered his head and kissed her. Khalil had only meant for it to be a short goodbye kiss, but the moment their lips touched, fire swept through him and he could no more stop kissing her than he could stop breathing. He pulled her closer and deepened the kiss, tasting and teasing her tongue with his. The pressure of her against him caused a slight discomfort, but he ignored it for the time being.

At length, she tore her mouth away, her breathing as ragged as his. "I...I need to go." She pointed to the door.

His ribs might be broken, his wrist sprained and his hearing damaged, but one part of his body worked just fine. It wouldn't take much for him to drag her upstairs to his bedroom. He agreed. She needed to leave.

She opened the door and jumped back.

Khalil leaned around the door to see what happened and met his mother's smiling face. He cursed under his breath. "Hey, Mom," he said grimly. Khalil had always been careful to keep his liaisons or any women, for that matter, out of his mother's sight. She was on a mission to see all of her children married and with him being next in line age-wise, she'd turned her full attention to him. And now there would be no stopping her.

Lexia's gaze flew to Khalil's. Her heart still raced and her body trembled with desire. She had to get away from this man *now*.

"Mom, this is Lexia Daniels. Lexia, my mother, DeAnna Gray."

"It's very nice to meet you, Mrs. Gray." She was tall, trim and, even wearing slacks, a faux wrap blouse and low-heeled pumps, she had the regal bearing of a queen.

"Same here, dear."

Khalil hugged his mother. "Come on in, Mom. Lexia was just leaving and I'm going to walk her down."

His mother swept in and latched onto Lexia's arm. "Oh,

honey, you don't have to leave on my account. In fact, why don't you stay?" She held up a bag. "I brought Khalil some dinner and there's plenty."

The fragrant smell of fried chicken wafted to her nose. Lexia smiled and shook her head. "Thank you so much for the offer, but I don't want to intrude. I just stopped by for a few minutes."

"Nonsense." She closed the door and gestured them to the kitchen.

Khalil sighed.

Lexia glanced over her shoulder at him as she followed his mother and he gave her an apologetic look.

After depositing the bag on the counter, his mother went back and scanned the living room.

"What are you looking for, Mom?" She pantomimed a phone. Khalil stepped around her and picked them up from the love seat, where he and Lexia had left them. He handed it to his mother and she immediately grilled him with rapid-fire questions: Why hadn't he told her about Lexia? How long had they been dating…?

Lexia's eyes widened. "Mrs. Gray, Khalil and I are not dating. I happened to be there the day he got hurt and just wanted to see how he was doing."

His mother's smile widened. "Oh, you're the one Brandon told me about." She threw her arms around Lexia and engulfed her in a smothering hug. "Thank you so much for being there with him. I've been wanting to meet you." She brought her hands together. "This is so wonderful!"

Lexia groaned inwardly. She hazarded a glance Khalil's way. The look on his face was a mixture of irritation and resignation. Despite Lexia's continued protests, Mrs. Gray went about setting plates, silverware and the food on the table.

Khalil came and stood close to her. "Sorry about this," he whispered.

"It's okay," she mouthed.

Mrs. Gray waved them over and made sure she brought the cell phones with her.

Khalil seated them both, and then took the chair opposite Lexia.

"Khalil, can you bless the food, please?"

He read the screen, bowed his head and recited a short blessing.

Everyone filled their plates with fried chicken, mashed potatoes and green beans and for the first few minutes the only sounds were that of forks scraping against plates. The fried chicken almost made Lexia moan it was so good. She really wanted to ask about the seasoning, but figured it would only give his mother more ammunition for her matchmaking, so she refrained.

"Lexia, Brandon says you own the café at the office," Mrs. Gray said.

"Yes, ma'am. It's hard work, but I really enjoy it."

"Isn't that something? You and Khalil both own a business."

"Mine is pretty small compared to Khalil's and your family's home safety company. How did you all get into that business?" Lexia asked, steering the conversation away from her.

Mrs. Gray launched into an explanation of her husband's frustration with getting equipment and accommodations for the disabled, his designing the equipment in their garage and subsequently starting the company. "And after more than two decades, he finally turned the reins over to Brandon almost a year ago."

"That's a great story." They had accomplished a lot in those years. "It seems as though creativity runs in your family. Khalil mentioned designing equipment for his fitness center." Though he didn't comment, she noticed him following the conversation on his screen.

"He's the most creative of my five children. Has he shown you his paintings?"

Paintings? "No." To him she asked, "What kinds of things do you paint?"

Khalil's eyes met hers. "People, cars and, every now and then, landscapes."

She remembered seeing a painting of a sunset when they were upstairs. "Did you paint the sunset that's on the wall in your bedroom?" As soon as the words were off her tongue, she wanted to snatch them back. His mother divided a speculative look between Lexia and Khalil, and Lexia wanted to slide under the table.

He must have seen Lexia's expression because he quickly offered an explanation. "I gave Lexia a tour when she got here," he said to his mother. And, yes. I painted it a few years ago."

"It's beautiful. You're very talented."

Still smiling at them, his mother said, "I agree."

Lexia hurriedly finished her food. "Thank you so much for dinner, Mrs. Gray. I really should be going now. I have to be at the café before five in the morning."

"Oh my. That's early."

She chuckled. "Yes, it is." She stood and picked up her plate.

Khalil lifted his hand. "Leave it. I'll take care of it." He rose to his feet, came around to her side and offered his hand.

She stared at his outstretched hand for a moment before taking it and allowing him to help her up. She wanted to tell him that his chivalry wasn't helping to dispel the notion that they were dating. Lexia turned toward his mother. "It was very nice meeting you. Thank you, again."

"You're welcome. We're having a family dinner on Sunday. Khalil, you should bring Lexia, so your father can meet her."

Lexia stopped midstep. "I…um…"

Khalil took one look at Lexia's face and leaned down to see what his mother had said. His eyes widened. "Mom—"

"Didn't you tell me the doctor said you could drive?"

His jaw tightened. "Yes, but—"

Even though he would never say it, Lexia knew he was afraid to drive. "Mrs. Gray, I appreciate the offer, but I already have plans for Sunday."

The older woman looked crestfallen. "Well, okay. Maybe some other time."

"Perhaps. Have a good evening."

"You do the same, Lexia."

"I'm going to walk her out, Mom. I'll be right back." Khalil grabbed his keys off a wall hook. He waited until they were at the elevator before speaking. "I'm really sorry about my mother. She's on a serious kick to get us all married off. So every time my brother Malcolm or I say hello to a woman in passing, she starts her matchmaking campaign."

"It's okay." She typed a message and held it up. "You don't have to walk me out. I can find my way back down."

"I know. But humor me." The elevator doors opened and he gestured her in.

They stopped twice to pick up passengers and each time, Khalil moved closer to Lexia. The heat of his body surrounded her, making her remember their earlier kiss—the way his mouth moved slowly over hers and how his hands traveled up and down her body. She tried to create some space between them, but was flush against the wall with nowhere to go. She breathed a sigh of relief when they got to the lobby. He reached for her hand and escorted her out to the valet. She gave the man her guest ticket.

It took only a minute for him to return with her car. Khalil walked around to the driver's side with her, brushed a kiss over her lips and closed the door behind her. She drove off, unable to get the feel of his kiss off her mind. Being with him reminded her of what she'd been missing. Things better left alone. But she didn't seem to be able to stop the thoughts.

Chapter 9

Khalil sat in his usual spot at the family Sunday dinner observing all the conversations and laughter flowing. He found out in the first five minutes that using the app was useless with ten people around the table. For the most part, he felt isolated—almost invisible. He tried to read their lips to pick up small bits of what they were saying, but had a difficult time. One, lipreading was much harder than he anticipated, and two, for the first time, he realized that they never really looked at each other when they spoke.

Everyone kept trying to do things for him that he could do himself, despite his protests, and the longer he sat, the more frustrated he became and started to withdraw into himself. His appetite disappeared and he found himself pushing the food around his plate instead of eating it. Not able to take it any longer, he excused himself and went out to the back deck. A short while later, Khalil felt a hand on his shoulder.

"Are you all right, son? You didn't eat much." His father handed him the cell phone.

"Yeah. Just frustrated."

"Forgive us for not making sure you could follow the conversation." He shook his head and a pained expression crossed his face. "I forget sometimes."

Khalil wished he could forget, too. "I know, Dad."

"Your mother wants to postpone the cruise and I think it might be a good idea."

"You don't need to do that. I told Mom the same thing. I'm going to work tomorrow." He had planned to go one day last week, but changed his mind because, although the drive would only take him about fifteen minutes, he wasn't ready to get on the road. Thankfully, nothing else had happened and Malcolm and Alonzo had kept him updated. He had ridden over with Omar and Morgan today, but he had to get past this fear.

"Are you sure you're ready to do that? Your ribs and wrist are still healing and you shouldn't be running around a gym all day."

"I won't be running around. I'll be sitting in my office. All of my personal training clients have been scheduled with my staff for this week and, as much as it's killing me not to, I won't be lifting any weights. So go on your cruise. You and Mom have been waiting a long time to do this and deserve this time together after sacrificing all these years."

"If you're sure."

"I am. I had my telephone equipment installed, so if you call, I'll be able to answer."

"Good enough, then. Come on in and have some dessert. Your mama made your favorite peach cobbler."

Khalil grinned. "I'll be in in a minute." He stayed outside a few minutes longer, then steeled himself for more of his mother's hovering. She had stayed over at his house for another two hours last week after Lexia left and no amount of pleading had moved her. She'd brought word search puzzles, a romance novel and ample snacks. If she hadn't had scheduled appointments for the rest of the week, she probably would have come back to camp out on his sofa. Another reason for him to go to work. He was tired of them treating him like an invalid. *Then stop acting like one*, an inner voice said. "I'm trying," he muttered and went inside.

His father must have said something because his siblings seemed to go out of their way to include him in conversations and spoke one at a time so he could keep up and they all downloaded the speech app on their phones.

Khalil found that he relaxed a little. However, by the time he made it home, being up and out had taken a toll on him and he was in bed by nine.

The next morning, the closer it came to the time for him to leave, the more anxious he became. His heart pounded in his chest and his hands shook as he got behind the wheel of the car. He toyed with texting Felicia and telling her he wouldn't be in, but she'd been filling in for him long enough and keeping tabs on Logan, going far above her normal duties. He had also scheduled a meeting with Alonzo to view the videos he had recorded.

Khalil left his complex and merged into the sparse traffic. As he continued, more cars filled the streets and his heart rate increased and his breath came in short gasps. He kept checking his mirrors and found himself driving at least ten miles below the speed limit. He became so uneasy that he had to pull off the road for a minute. He leaned against the headrest and waited for his breathing to slow and his heart rate to return to normal.

"You can do this," he repeated over and over. "It's only a fifteen-minute drive." He'd been driving since he was fifteen and had never gotten one traffic violation. He kept up with his pep talk for a good five minutes and, when he felt in control, continued to the gym. By the time Khalil parked in his spot, he was sweating as if it was a hundred degrees instead of sixty. He took a moment to compose himself and got out of the car.

As soon as he walked through the door, several members stopped their workouts and turned his way. The day receptionist jumped from her seat, came around the desk, hesitated briefly, and then hugged him. "Hey, Chantel." She had on a black T-shirt with the gym's logo and a pair of gray leggings.

Her mouth started moving rapidly, and then she paused and clamped a hand over her mouth. Chantel reached for a notepad and pen. She held it up. *Sorry.*

"It's okay. I'm going up to my office. I'm expecting Alonzo Wright at ten. Just send him up when he gets here." In his peripheral vision he noticed people still staring.

She nodded.

Khalil threw up a wave as he passed through the gym and made his way to the elevator that would take him to the second floor. He usually took the stairs, but not today. He'd been trying to wean himself off the pain medication and didn't take any last night. As a result, his pain levels were up and he planned to cut his workday short and go home after his meeting with Alonzo in a couple of hours.

Upstairs, he unlocked his office and scanned the room to see if anything had been moved. He checked his desk and saw that a stack of papers he'd left on the right had been moved slightly toward the middle. Had Logan come into the office another time? Felicia appeared in the doorway with tears in her eyes. Just like Chantel, Felicia seemed unsure of what to do. She waved and wrung her hands. "I'm okay, so don't go getting all emotional."

Felicia thrust a piece of paper at him.

He took it and read. "Thanks. I'm glad it wasn't worse, too." He'd brought the cell phones to make it easier to talk to everyone and explained to her how they worked. His family had all downloaded the app on their phones, but he still carried this one for the times he had to meet with other people.

"So I just talk and whatever I say will appear on your phone?"

"Yep." He showed her his phone.

"Wow. I had no idea this kind of technology existed."

Neither had Khalil. And he still wouldn't if the explosion never happened. "Has Logan tried to get in my office since we talked?"

"I don't think so, but he was too mad after I locked the door." Felicia placed a hand on her hip. "He kept trying to tell me that since you were out and he was the manager, he needed to have access to the office to keep things running in your absence. I told him he could do the same thing from his little office." She rolled her eyes. "He must think I was born yesterday."

He chuckled. Felicia hadn't liked Logan from the first. He assumed because he was the manager that he should be the only person, aside from Khalil, with full access. But Khalil didn't give full access to anyone. The only reason he hadn't given the position to Felicia was because of her school and study schedule. She was also a certified trainer and had only two clients for the same reason. But she would be graduating with her master's in biokinesiology from USC in a few months and he planned to promote her and have her manage the new gym, or this one if it turned out that Logan was behind stealing from the gym's members. "I'll have a talk with him before I leave today."

"Are you staying all day?"

"No. I'm leaving after my meeting this morning, but I'll be back tomorrow. Malcolm is going to come in for a few hours this week, as well." His brother had agreed to keep an eye on things for the next two or three weeks until Khalil could handle a full schedule.

Felicia's eyes lit up and she smiled. "Well, now."

She'd had a crush on Malcolm for the past year, but Malcolm had made it clear to Khalil he wasn't interested. After having his heart broken by his college sweetheart, Malcolm swore he would never date another woman seriously. Khalil understood and agreed. Memories of his betrayal surfaced in his mind, but he pushed them aside. "How's your thesis coming?"

"I'm three-quarters of the way done. I have a meeting with my advisor tomorrow, so I'll need to leave early."

"No problem."

"I know you have a lot to catch up on, so I'll let you get to it."

"Okay. I'll let you know when I'm leaving."

She handed the cell back and walked out.

Khalil sat at his desk and went through all the mail that had accumulated over the past two weeks and cleared out his emails. He had just finished when Alonzo arrived. He explained, once again, about the speech app.

Alonzo pulled out his own cell. "I'll just download it on my phone, so you don't have to keep passing around that one." Once he'd done it, he said, "I've been tracking your computer and I don't know if Malcolm told you, but no one's logged on except you."

"He told me."

"But there were a couple of things on the cameras I think you should see." Alonzo turned on his iPad and handed it to Khalil.

He watched the footage from three days ago. Logan was standing outside of Khalil's office jiggling the knob. His face registered anger when he found the door locked. He glanced up and down the hallway and squatted down in front of the knob as if he were trying to figure out a way to get in. He finally rose and headed back the way he had come. "Is this the only time he's been up here?"

"There's one more two weeks ago. Click on Tuesday."

Khalil did as asked and saw the confrontation between Logan and Felicia. Logan was standing behind Khalil's desk and Felicia just inside the doorway. The argument lasted a minute before Logan stormed out. Then Felicia locked the door. This must have been the day she called him right before the explosion. "Is there anything I can do? If Logan is the one doing this, I want him gone."

"Right now we don't have any proof, so it might be hard to fire him."

"So, what? I wait?"

"For the time being. He seems pretty arrogant, and people like him will slip up. Besides, he has no idea he's being tracked. So that works in our favor."

He didn't want to wait. The fact that the man had tried to get into Khalil's office made it hard not to fire him on the spot. But Alonzo was right. "All right. I'll wait. Thanks, Alonzo."

Alonzo stood and handed him a card. "Here's the code to access the cameras. I figure you want to check it out yourself now."

"I do. I'll call you if I see anything."

"And I'll do the same."

Khalil drummed his fingers on the desk. He hoped for Logan's sake that he'd done nothing. If he did, Khalil planned to whip his ass. He went downstairs to Logan's office.

When Logan looked up and saw Khalil, he started scribbling on paper.

"You don't have to write—we can use these. Just talk in this phone and I'll see it on mine."

"It's good you're back, man. Felicia's been acting like she's in charge."

"She mentioned you going in my office. I'm not sure why because there's nothing in there that you'd need."

Logan's eyes widened for a split second. "I…um… One of your clients came in and wanted to know your schedule. I was just checking to see when their appointment was in case I needed to shift him to one of the other trainers because I didn't know when you were going to be back."

The man was definitely up to something. None of Khalil's personal training clients would have come in because he'd had Felicia cancel them the first week. The second week the other trainers had worked with them. But Logan wouldn't know that because his job was to make sure the equipment functioned properly, schedule routine maintenance, and take care of marketing. "I'll take care of my schedule, so there won't be a need for you to worry about being in my office. Has all the maintenance of the machines been scheduled?"

"Not yet, but I'll have it done today."

"Email me the list when it's done."

He nodded tightly.

"I'll see you tomorrow." Khalil held his hand out for the phone. He had planned to ask Logan to take care of payroll tomorrow, but he didn't trust the man and decided he'd do it himself. He was going to have Alonzo come back and install a camera in Logan's office.

He poked his head in Felicia's office to let her know he was leaving and gave himself another pep talk for the drive home. This time he made it without having to stop, but his steps were slow as he trekked down the hallway to his condo. Once inside, he eased himself down on the sofa and stretched out.

Before Khalil could get comfortable, his cell buzzed. *Please don't let this be my mother.* She'd taken to texting him every day, sometimes more than once. He dug it out of his pocket and saw Gerald Walters's name on the display. The agent had been in the business for more than two decades and had launched the careers of several models. Though he hadn't been Khalil's agent, Gerald had recommended Khalil for a few assignments that had kept him in the limelight for years.

Khalil read the message and frowned. The man had heard about the accident and thought it best that he find another escort for Rosalyn just in case Khalil hadn't recovered from his injuries.

Khalil: The fund-raiser isn't for another three weeks and I'm sure I'll be fine.

Gerald: What about your other injuries?

Khalil: I have three broken ribs and a sprained wrist. Hardly life threatening.

Gerald: I was talking about your other injury.

It finally dawned on Khalil what he meant. Are you referring to my hearing loss?

Gerald: Yes. With all the networking required, I'm not sure—

He didn't bother to read the rest of the message. So, because he couldn't hear, he could no longer be considered a valuable part of a community to which he'd given over ten years of his life. Not to mention that *he* started the youth program after seeing the toll the grueling schedule was taking on some of the younger models. He'd developed mentorships and encouraged them to balance modeling with school because they'd need to have a skill after leaving the business. The fund-raiser raised money for college scholarships and lodging assistance for parents traveling with their teen. But none of that mattered now.

White-hot rage swept through him, magnifying his pain. His ears were ringing, head pounding and ribs aching. He gritted his teeth and clenched his fists. As much as he didn't want to take the pain medication, he knew he'd have to take it; otherwise he'd never get any rest. Maybe if he lay there for a while, the pain would subside. He didn't like the way the medication clouded his mind, but after thirty minutes he finally relented.

Two hours later, Khalil awoke from a nap and sent up a prayer of thanks that the intense aching in his head and body had dulled considerably. However, just the thought of Gerald's texts raised it a notch. He forced it out of his mind, braced himself and sat up. The bright green bag holding the book that Lexia had brought over last week still sat undisturbed on the coffee table. Even now, he couldn't believe that she knew sign language or that she had learned it just to be able to talk to her friend.

He took the book out and flipped through the pages. She'd said it had taken her over three years to become proficient. *Please don't let it take that long for me to recover my hearing.* He read a few pages and tried to make the first few letters of the alphabet, but gave up in less than five minutes. He could not do this. *I'll help you in any way I can.* Lexia's words came back to him. Would she really help him? And did he want to learn? He still was somewhat hesitant, but he'd take any excuse to see her again.

He grabbed his cell phone. Hey, Lexia. A few minutes passed, then his phone buzzed.

Lexia: Hey. How are you feeling?

Khalil: Better. Did you take classes to learn sign language?

Lexia: A couple. Are you going to do it?

Khalil: Only if you teach me.

   Minutes passed before she responded: I'm not a teacher.

Khalil: But you said you'd help me in any way you can. And this is how you can help me.

Lexia: That's not what I meant.

Khalil: Maybe not, but that's what you said. So, will you help me?

Lexia: I'll agree on one condition, that you put in the time studying.

   He had to think about that for a long moment. He recalled how frustrated he became when trying to learn French and, after leafing through the sign language book, could see the same thing happening.

Lexia: Well?

   Khalil's thumbs hovered over the screen's keyboard. Okay.

Lexia: When do you want to start?

Khalil: Tonight, if you're not busy.

Lexia: Let's make it tomorrow afternoon. Oh, and I think we should just focus on the ASL for now.

Khalil: No promises.

Lexia: What does that mean?

Khalil: It means that the first chance I get I'm going to take my time touching you, tasting you and kissing you. Any other questions?

Lexia: See you tomorrow.

If she thought he'd be able to sit next to her and ignore the chemistry between them, she had another think coming. No, he wasn't interested in anything permanent, but he didn't see anything wrong with the two of them exploring this mutual attraction.

Chapter 10

Lexia muttered to herself all the way down the hallway leading to Khalil's condo Tuesday afternoon. Yes, she had promised to help him, but the man had no problems twisting her words to his benefit. *Stick to the plan, Lexia. Focus on fingerspelling the alphabet and not his captivating eyes, smooth as honey voice and warm, sexy lips.* She groaned. Who was she kidding? Her lips tingled at the prospect of him kissing her again. She stopped at the door and sent him a text. A moment later, it swung open. She did her best to keep her eyes focused on his face and not the corded muscles of his arms and chest visible beneath the sleeveless tee. Then again, with his newly trimmed mustache and beard, long eyelashes and golden-brown-sugar eyes, his face was just as much a visual treat as the rest of his body.

Khalil's low chuckle snapped her out of her thoughts. "Come on in."

He backed up just enough so that when she passed their bodies brushed against each other, the contact sending a jolt of awareness through her. Lexia stifled a moan. Halfway across the room, she turned around and noticed him standing with his back braced against the door, arms folded. She angled her head. "What?" He straightened and came toward her with the grace of a panther and she unconsciously took a step back.

Khalil stroked a finger down her cheek. "I didn't get my hello kiss."

Before Lexia could blink, his mouth came down on hers, hot and demanding. His mouth devoured hers and she came up on her toes and slid her arms around his neck to pull him closer.

He groaned and trailed kisses along her jaw, behind her ear and in the hollow of her throat.

Her body trembled and she moaned his name. Fighting for control, she released him and moved out of his embrace. She pointed to the book lying on the table and sat on the sofa.

He nodded and took a seat next to her. "What's first?"

"We'll start with learning the alphabet. The signs pictured in the book are for right-handed people, but since you're left-handed you'll just make them in reverse. Ready?"

"I guess."

Lexia smiled at his less than enthusiastic response. "Let's do the first five letters." She demonstrated each letter, saying it aloud and waiting for him repeat it. They practiced over and over. "Okay, now I'm going to call out a letter randomly and you show it to me—*D*."

Khalil sat for a moment as if thinking, then made the correct letter.

"Right." He got five out of five and they moved to the next five. The added letters proved to be more of a challenge and she had to help him with some of the hand positions.

"I can't get this," he grumbled.

"It's only your first time and we've been at it for what, fifteen minutes? Of course you aren't going to get them all right away."

Khalil let out an exasperated sigh. "Keep going."

They continued for another fifteen minutes. "How about we stop here? Just practice them every day and add more as you feel comfortable."

He closed the book and tossed it onto the table. "How do people do this?"

"With lots of practice. I told you it took me over three

years to become fluent, but I could hold a very basic conversation after about a year and a half. Hopefully, your hearing will return long before then," she added when he frowned.

He leaned forward and cradled his head in his hands. "Every day I wake up, praying that I'll hear some sound… *anything*, but there's nothing. Absolutely nothing," he said emotionally.

Lexia placed a comforting hand on his back. She didn't know what to say and didn't want to trivialize his pain, so she kept quiet.

Finally, he raised his head. "So what do you want to do now?"

She hadn't planned on doing anything other than getting him started and leaving. "I don't know. I wasn't going to stay long. A movie?" She had momentarily forgotten about his hearing and said the first thing that came to her mind.

Khalil scowled. "A movie? I can't watch a movie."

She lifted a brow. "Why not? There's nothing wrong with your eyes. And, unless you have a television built in 1950, it should have captions." Lexia studied him. "Are you telling me that you haven't turned your TV on in two weeks?" His expression said it all.

"Why turn it on if I can't hear what's going on?"

"Again, captions. But if you don't want to watch one, that's fine."

"No, no…okay."

Lexia smiled. "Great. Do you have any popcorn?"

"I think so." Khalil stood, went to the kitchen and searched the cabinets and walk-in pantry. He held up a box of microwave popcorn.

She joined him and took out two packages.

"We don't need two."

Lexia cut him a look. "We do if you want some. I do not share my popcorn. So, are you having some?"

He nodded. "Anything else, Your Highness?"

"Tea?"

Khalil pulled out a drawer. "What kind?"

She peered into the drawer and burst out laughing. He had at least twenty varieties of tea. "I guess you like tea, huh?"

He shrugged. "I don't drink coffee and I don't like a lot of caffeine, so…"

She scanned the selections and settled on mango passion fruit herbal tea.

"Do you want it hot or cold?"

"Hot, please."

He filled the kettle with water and set it on the stove to heat, then started the popcorn in the microwave.

Lexia sat on a stool at the bar and observed him in the kitchen. He seemed quite comfortable. She could count on one hand the number of times her ex stepped foot into the kitchen to prepare something. Not even popcorn. He always had a ready excuse as to why he couldn't do it. That was one more reason her short marriage came to an end. When everything was done, he dumped the bags of popcorn into large bowls. She added a little sugar to her tea, grabbed a bowl and followed him out. He bypassed the living room and continued to the stairs. Was he planning for them to watch TV in his bedroom? That would be dangerous on every level. Sure enough he headed directly there. She hovered in the doorway.

Khalil set his bowl and mug of tea on the table by the fireplace. "Make yourself comfortable. I'll be right back."

Make herself comfortable? Because of its position, they could only view the television from his bed. And that's the last place she needed to be. Lexia hadn't moved from her spot when he returned with two trays and napkins.

"Problems?" he asked, placing the trays down and retrieving his snacks. He climbed onto the bed and patted the space next to him.

She tentatively approached the large bed. She put the bowl of popcorn on the tray, the tea on the nightstand and sat, leaving plenty of space between them. "What are we watching?"

"I've been meaning to watch *The Magnificent Seven* for months, so that's what's in the player, but we can choose something else if you don't want to see it."

"Me, turn down a movie with Denzel in it? Please."

Khalil smiled, shook his head and started the movie.

Lexia picked up the remote and turned the sound down.

"What are you doing? Did I have it too loud?"

"Nope. I'm going to watch it with the captions, just like you."

He gave her a strange look, then leaned over and placed a soft kiss on her lips. "You're a special lady, Lexia."

They shared a smile and settled in. She had never been a huge fan of westerns, but Denzel and Chris Pratt had her eyes glued to the screen. She wanted the villain dead now, not two hours from now. She and Khalil laughed and commented on scenes and had a great time.

"Mmm, mmm, that Denzel is one good-looking man."

"I don't know what all you women see in him. He's old enough to be your father."

Lexia paused with a fistful of popcorn and gave Khalil a look of disbelief. "So what. The man is still sexy as all get out."

Khalil shook his head. "So, is that what you look for in a man, his sex appeal?"

"Of course not, but I do want the package to look good."

"Sounds a little judgmental to me," he said with a teasing glint in his eye, reminding her of when she'd said the same thing to him. "There could be a nice guy beneath all that bad packaging."

Her mouth dropped. She threw a handful of popcorn at him. "Shut up and watch the movie."

He threw his head back and laughed. "I couldn't resist." He wrapped a hand around his middle and groaned, but kept laughing.

She rolled her eyes, scooted as far away from him as she could without falling off the bed and skewered him with a look. "See if I watch another movie with you." She bit her lip to keep her smile hidden and refocused on the movie.

"That was a good movie," Khalil said as the credits rolled on the screen. "Much better than I anticipated."

"It was. I'm still a little salty about some of the parts, though." The room had darkened considerably and the sun had started its descent. The view from his window tempted her to ask if they could sit out there to watch it, but she thought it best they got out of his bed and out of this room.

Apparently he'd read her mind. "Let's go check out the sunset. Unless you have other plans for the evening."

It was on the tip of her tongue to lie and say she did, but she couldn't bring herself to do it. "Nothing other than cooking dinner and doing some menu planning."

Khalil eased off the bed and grabbed the same blanket they'd used the last time. "Well, I'll cook you dinner, so that'll be one thing off your list."

"Oh, you don't have to do that," Lexia said quickly.

"I know, but since you took time out of your schedule to come and help me out, it's the least I can do. Besides, I want to make up for my rude behavior the other day."

The sting of his words came back to her, but she pushed them away because she understood his frustration. "Okay."

Out on the balcony, he wrapped her in the blanket and held her the same way as last time. A short while later, his hands started roaming up and down her thighs, over her torso and up to cup her breasts. Lexia gasped. His lips skated along her temple, down her cheek and ended at her mouth. "Khalil." His name slipped from her lips. He shifted her and continued kissing her body.

"I've wanted to touch you and kiss you like this from the moment you walked through my door," he murmured.

Lexia had wanted the same, but couldn't tell him that. She stilled when he dipped his hand inside her loose sweatpants, squeezed her buttocks, moved around to the front and slid her panties to the side. He parted her folds and his skilled fingers went to work on her. Moans spilled from her throat.

"Lift your leg over mine," he whispered against her lips.

She complied and his fingers sank deeper, sending shock waves of pleasure through her. He teased her slowly at first, increased the speed and then took up the unhurried pace again. Each time he brought her closer to the edge and she cried out. The sensations heightened and she gripped his shirtfront as a blinding orgasm tore through her. He seemed to sense she was about to scream and covered her mouth with his. Her body trembled and she gasped for air.

At length, he removed his hand, but continued to kiss her.

Finally, he lifted his head. The blatant desire she read in his eyes rekindled her passion. She ran a caressing hand down his bearded face and over the strength of his arms. She slid her hands beneath his tee, wanting to touch his warm, bare skin and feel the muscles flex and contract under her touch. She heard his sharp intake of breath and resumed her journey, being careful not to injure him. Lexia felt herself losing control and couldn't do anything to stop it. Didn't want to stop it.

* * *

Khalil relished the feeling of Lexia's hand on his body. He couldn't explain why her touch sparked something within him he'd never experienced before. Ignoring the slight discomfort in his upper body and hand, he shifted her until she was stretched out next to him on the wide lounger. Thankfully, the balcony had privacy walls on either side. Being on the top floor was an added bonus, so they were shielded from prying eyes. He lifted her top and bent his head to kiss the tops of her breasts visible above her bra. As he'd told her yesterday, he wanted to taste, touch and kiss her. The way her feminine muscles clamped down on his fingers had him ready to take things to the next level.

He reached around and unclasped her bra and eased the cups to the side, baring her breasts to him. Khalil latched on to one dark nipple and sucked gently. He felt the vibrations and knew she was saying something. He loved her voice and missed it and, more than anything, he wanted to hear her sounds of pleasure. Hear her scream his name when he made her come again. He was quickly losing control and, although parts of his body were in full agreement, the pain in his ribs let him know it wouldn't happen tonight.

Khalil raised his head, traced her kiss-swollen lips and lowered his head. Her taste was intoxicating and he had to force himself to back away. He sat up, pulled her with him and helped redo her clothing. He gave her one last kiss. "Come on so I can feed you, baby." He guided her to his bathroom, where she could clean up. He used the spare one and came back just as she finished.

Together, they made their way downstairs and he took out the chicken breasts that he had marinating in a chipotle lime mix, red and yellow bell peppers and an onion.

Lexia placed a hand on his arm and fingerspelled.

FREE Merchandise is 'in the Cards' for you!

Dear Reader,

We're giving away FREE MERCHANDISE!

Seriously, we'd like to reward you for reading this novel by giving you **FREE MERCHANDISE** worth over **$20** retail. And no purchase is necessary!

You see the Jack of Hearts sticker above? Paste that sticker in the box on the Free Merchandise Voucher inside. Return the Voucher today... and we'll send you Free Merchandise!

Thanks again for reading one of our novels—and enjoy your Free Merchandise with our compliments!

Pam Powers

Pam Powers

P.S. Look inside to see what Free Merchandise is **"in the cards"** for you!

We'd like to send you two free books like the one you are enjoying now. Your two books have a combined cover price of over $10 retail, but they are yours to keep absolutely FREE! We'll even send you 2 wonderful surprise gifts. You can't lose!

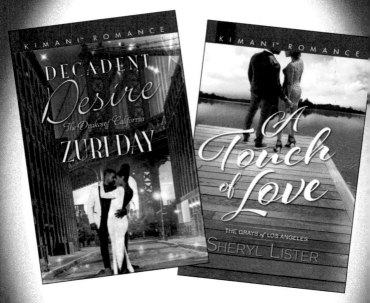

REMEMBER: Your Free Merchandise, consisting of **2 Free Books** and **2 Free Gifts**, is worth over $20 retail! No purchase is necessary, so please send for your Free Merchandise today.

Get TWO FREE GIFTS!
We'll also send you 2 wonderful FREE GIFTS (worth about $10 retail), in addition to your 2 Free books!

Visit us at:
www.ReaderService.com

Books received may not be as shown.

YOUR FREE MERCHANDISE INCLUDES...
2 FREE Books **AND** 2 FREE Mystery Gifts

FREE MERCHANDISE VOUCHER

2 FREE BOOKS and **2 FREE GIFTS**

Please send my Free Merchandise, consisting of
2 Free Books and **2 Free Mystery Gifts**.
I understand that I am under no obligation to buy
anything, as explained on the back of this card.

168/368 XDL GMWC

Please Print

FIRST NAME

LAST NAME

ADDRESS

APT.#   CITY

STATE/PROV.   ZIP/POSTAL CODE

NO PURCHASE NECESSARY!

K-N17-FFM17

READER SERVICE—Here's how it works:

▲ If offer card is missing write to: Reader Service, P.O. Box 1341, Buffalo, NY 14240-8531 or visit www.ReaderService.com ▲

BUSINESS REPLY MAIL

FIRST-CLASS MAIL   PERMIT NO. 717   BUFFALO, NY

POSTAGE WILL BE PAID BY ADDRESSEE

READER SERVICE
PO BOX 1341
BUFFALO NY 14240-8571

NO POSTAGE
NECESSARY
IF MAILED
IN THE
UNITED STATES

F-a-j-i-t-a-s. Or that's what he thought it was. They hadn't gotten to the end of the alphabet. "Fajitas?"

She smiled, nodded and twisted her hands back and forth in the air.

"That's a sign for…?"

She clapped.

"Applause?"

This time, she raised her closed fist and bent it up and down at the wrist. He lifted a brow.

"Yes," she mouthed.

"So this is applause or clapping and this means yes." Khalil repeated the signs.

"Very good."

"I'm glad you think so. So far I've got yes, clapping and about half of ten letters down. Not real competent." He sensed that this would be much harder than learning French or Spanish. "To answer your question, yes, I'm making fajitas. Is that okay with you?"

"Sounds good. I can help, if you want. Just tell me what you want me to do."

He leaned down to read what she'd said. "Unlike my sign language skills, I'm pretty competent in the kitchen, so you can hang out on the terrace or take a seat at the bar and keep me company." Their eyes held, then she climbed up onto a bar stool. "Can I get you anything while you're waiting?"

"No, thanks. I'm going to check my email."

"Go right ahead." Khalil got out a large cutting board and sliced the vegetables. He preheated the built-in grill on his stove and added the chicken. While it cooked, he sautéed the peppers and onion. He thought about opening a bottle of wine, but decided against it because he continued to intermittently take the pain medication. He made lemonade, instead.

He stole glances at Lexia as she typed on her phone.

She was the first woman he'd invited to his home, outside of the few times he had hosted get-togethers for friends. However, he hadn't been romantically interested in any of those women. His relationships, if they could be termed as such, never lasted past three or four dates and he preferred it that way because no one got hurt. He tried to apply the same logistics to his relationship with Lexia, but was having difficulties maintaining the distance he usually craved.

Khalil placed the now-done chicken on a plate to rest, filled small bowls with cheese and sour cream and placed them on the table. He warmed the flour tortillas, sliced the chicken and added them to a plate, along with the peppers. "Dinner's ready," he said, passing Lexia.

Lexia hopped off the stool, picked up the pitcher of lemonade and followed him to the table.

"Let me get glasses and we'll be all set." He came back, filled their glasses and sat across from her. He gestured to the food. "Ladies first." She didn't move. "What's wrong?"

She rose and got her cell phone. "I was waiting for you to bless the food. Or do you only do that when your mom is here?"

He grinned sheepishly. "I do it most times." Khalil quickly said a blessing. They filled their plates and ate in silence for the first couple of minutes. He didn't talk much because he was tired of stopping to read a message. He just wanted to talk *normally* for a change.

She held up her half-eaten fajita. "It's good."

"Thanks."

"What did you marinade the chicken in?"

He finished chewing and took a couple of sips of his lemonade. "It's a dry rub I made with ground chipotle peppers, cumin, paprika, salt, pepper and I added lime juice and some cilantro."

"I may need to borrow this recipe for the café. I'd give you credit, of course," she added with a smile.

Khalil chuckled. "You might want to hold off on that because it's not anything I've written down and I don't know the exact measurements. And I thought you already had a set menu."

Lexia wiped her hands. "I do, but I'm always looking for some new items to add, either permanently or seasonal. Right now, I'm exploring adding items that are leaning toward the healthier side and these grilled chicken breasts fall right in line. I guess I'd have to leave off all the cheese and sour cream, though."

"Probably."

"Changing subjects on you. Are you working tomorrow?"

"I'm going in for about three hours in the afternoon, why?"

"I'd like to take you to visit my friend, Elyse."

He went still. "The one who's deaf?"

She nodded hesitantly.

His first thought was a resounding *no*, but he'd promised himself he would make an effort to deal with this thing.

"It'll only be for an hour or so, maybe less. She has access to far more resources and can answer any questions you may have."

"Okay, I'll meet you there. I need to be at the gym by noon."

"If we met at ten, would that give you enough time to get back?"

"Plenty of time. Just text me the address. Can you be gone from the café that long?"

"Yep. It's after the morning rush and Sam and Jayla will be there. I should be back by the lunch rush to help, if needed." Lexia finished her food. "Thanks for dinner. Next time, it'll be my turn."

Next time meant that he'd get another opportunity to kiss her. "Just let me know when."

She glanced at her watch. "I can help you clean the kitchen before I leave."

Khalil stood. "Leave everything there and I'll take care of it when I get back."

She rose to her feet. "Why didn't you tell me you had someplace to go? I'm sorry."

He laughed. "The only place I'm going, sweet lady, is to follow you home."

She waved a hand dismissively. "I told you before you don't need to do that."

"Yep, you did. Let's go. And give me your address, just in case you decide to lose me on the road." Lexia doubled over in laughter and, again, he wished he could hear it.

When she composed herself, she pulled out her phone and sent a text. "I sent you my address and Elyse's."

"It's your real address, right?"

"Yes, you nut. Now, come on."

Downstairs, the valet brought both of their cars. Khalil still felt a little anxiety, especially since this would be the first time he'd driven at night. He took a deep breath and plugged Lexia's address into the GPS. He saw her friend's address and his mind shifted to tomorrow's visit. Once again, he battled with not wanting to go. He still held on to the belief that his condition would be very temporary, yet a small, nagging voice kept asking, *what if it's not?* Dr. Moyer had suggested Khalil talk to a counselor or psychologist to help him adjust, but Khalil refused to do that. With any luck, this visit would turn out to be beneficial.

Chapter 11

Wednesday morning, Khalil pulled up to the address Lexia had given him. He had assumed it would be a house, but was surprised to see a school—Sunny Coast School for the Deaf and Hard of Hearing. Was she trying to get him to take classes? His anger spiked. A moment later, Lexia came out of the building, smiling and waving at him. Her smile deflated some of his annoyance. He got out and met her halfway.

Lexia shielded her eyes from the sun. "I hope you found it okay."

He nodded. "Why are we here?"

"Because this is where Elyse is. She runs the school."

He felt his eyes widen. "She *runs* it?"

She signed, "Yes."

Curious, Khalil followed Lexia into a modern brick building. They passed several classrooms with colorful artwork on the doors and teachers standing in front of whiteboards. It looked like any other school. Finally, she escorted him into an office where a pretty, honey-brown-colored woman stood engaged in a conversation with a teenager. Their hands moved rapidly and the student nodded enthusiastically. The student waved and bounded out of the office.

The woman turned and noticed them. Her smile widened and she held her arms out to Lexia and they embraced.

Lexia reached for his hand and the cell and made introductions. "Khalil, this is my best friend, Elyse Ross. Elyse, this is Khalil Gray."

While Lexia held the phone, Elyse simultaneously spoke and signed, "I'm pleased to finally meet you, Khalil."

The smile on Elyse's face and the blush that crept over

Lexia's made him wonder what Lexia had told her friend. "Same here."

"Would you like a tour?"

"Yes." Khalil was impressed by the prekindergarten to twelfth grade school. The only difference was that the teachers and students used their hands to talk. On their way back to the office, he noticed a boy who looked to be about nine or ten, sitting alone on the playground with his arms folded. His steps slowed and he asked about the kid.

"That's Anthony. He's only been here about a month," Elyse explained. "He lost his hearing due to a virus six months ago and was struggling in school and getting into fights because the other students were teasing him. He refuses to learn sign language or use any of the technology because he's convinced his hearing will return soon."

His gaze went back to the sullen boy. What Elyse had described sounded exactly how Khalil felt.

"So far, none of us have been able to reach him, and we've tried everything from offering extra recess time to his favorite snacks, but..." She shrugged.

Elyse had mentioned during their tour that she could read lips. Khalil asked, "Do you mind if I give it a try?"

"Not at all."

"You might need this." Lexia handed him her cell phone.

"Thanks." He left the women standing there and made his way over to the bench where the boy sat. For several seconds, Khalil searched his mind for a way to start the conversation.

The kid scowled over at Khalil. "Who are you?"

He pointed to his ears, shook his head and handed his cell to the kid. "Mrs. Ross said you lost your hearing a few months ago. You're Anthony, right?" He pointed to the phone.

Anthony read the message and nodded.

"My name is Khalil Gray and I lost mine, too, a couple of weeks ago."

The boy whipped his head in Khalil's direction, surprise covering his face. "You did?"

Khalil nodded. "Yes. I'm pretty mad about it. I can't talk to my family and friends anymore without these." He held up the phone. "I can't listen to my favorite songs or my shows on TV."

Anthony switched phones. "That's how I feel. All my old friends were teasing me and they stopped inviting me to their houses and everything. I hate this."

"I know." The remembrance of Gerald's text came back to him. He'd heard about this type of discrimination, but had never experienced it, until now. He was the same person, his IQ hadn't changed, he still spoke three languages, yet the simple fact that he couldn't hear made him an outcast. "But I guess we're going to have to show our friends that we're still the same. I bet you're pretty smart in school."

His face lit up. "I had straight As on my report card at my old school."

"Then there's no reason that you can't do the same thing here."

Anthony's smile faded. "But what if I'm not smart enough. Everybody knows sign language except me."

"And me. I have to learn it, too, even though it seems pretty tough. And I bet you'll learn it faster than me."

He angled his head. "You think so?"

"I do. But you can only do that if you try. How about we make a deal to do our best?" Khalil stuck out his hand.

Anthony hesitated briefly before shaking the proffered hand. "Deal."

"Good. I have to go to work, but I'll be asking Mrs. Ross about how you're doing."

Anthony's eyes went wide. "You will?"

He signed, *yes*. "That means yes. Now, it's time for you to make some new friends."

His gaze went to the playground then back to Khalil. "I guess." He handed Khalil the cell, waved and left to join a group of students playing basketball. They immediately welcomed him.

Khalil smiled and stood. If only things could be that simple for him. He walked back to where Lexia and Elyse stood with their mouths hanging open.

Elyse immediately reached for the cell. "How did you do that?"

He glimpsed over his shoulder just in time to see Anthony make a basket and receive a high five from a teammate. He shrugged. "He just needed to talk to someone who understands. Can you let me know how he's doing?"

"You wouldn't by chance want a job here?"

Khalil laughed and shook his head. He and Lexia said their goodbyes and made their way out to the front of the school. He walked her to her car and, being mindful that they were at a school, gave her a short kiss. Lexia waved, got into her car and drove off. It was a good thing because the desire blazing in her dark eyes had tempted him to carry her off and find someplace to finish what they'd started last night. He'd wanted to spend the entire night making love to her, then wake up and do it all over again. He froze in his tracks. *Wake up and do it all again?* That implied her spending the night and he never did morning afters. *Ever.* Maybe he needed to step back. He needed to focus on getting himself back on track with the new fitness center opening, including hiring a manager and dealing with Logan. He had a feeling that he'd be firing the man soon. That meant he had no time for getting caught up in any kind of relationship. *Too late*, an inner voice said. Lexia had gotten to him.

* * *

Lexia sat in her office later thinking about Khalil and how he'd handled the student. There was so much more to him, she realized and found herself falling harder and harder. Last night he'd set her body on fire and she hadn't wanted him to stop. Visions of the encounter replayed in her mind and her eyes drifted closed. She could still feel the heat of his mouth on her breasts, the glide of his hand on her body and the intense climax.

"You okay, Lexia?"

Her eyes snapped open and she jerked upright in the chair. "Hey, Cam. Yeah, fine. What's up?"

Cam observed her. "You sure? That guy not giving you trouble, is he?"

Khalil was definitely giving her trouble, but not in the way Cam meant. "No."

"Okay. I just wanted to let you know that the guy is here to fix the window. I moved the tables and blocked off the area."

"Thanks. How's the job hunting going?"

He shrugged. "Feels like I've been out of the game a long time."

Lexia paused. "Are you okay?"

"It's nothing. I'm going out for a while."

"You're coming back, right?" She didn't want him to go back onto the streets.

"Yeah, Lexi. And don't even think about staying around until I do."

"I won't." Cam was a grown man and could make his own decisions and, as his friend, she needed to let him do it. It didn't stop her from being concerned, though. On the heels of his departure, Sam came in.

"You never said how things went with Khalil last night."

"They went okay. We started with the first ten letters of the alphabet."

"I'm not asking about that, and you know it. I want to know what happened *after* the lesson was over."

"We watched a movie then he cooked dinner—fajitas. I know you were going to ask." She had purposely left out the intimate parts.

Sam narrowed her eyes. "And he never kissed you once."

"I didn't say that. We…he…yes, he kissed me." And touched her in ways that made her want to throw caution to the wind.

She grinned. "Now we're getting somewhere. So, are you two dating exclusively?"

"No. And I don't think it's a good idea. In fact, now that he's doing better, I—"

"Don't even go there, Lexia. He hasn't done anything to deserve you cutting him off at the knees."

"I didn't say he did. But he's not looking for anything permanent, or temporary for that matter, and I don't want to be a convenient one-night stand for him. I know some women have no problems doing that. I'm just not one of them. I've never been good at separating my heart and body."

"You're falling for him."

Lexia didn't comment.

"For what it's worth, he seems like a good guy."

"He is."

"Give him a chance. Or at least let him mess up first," Sam added with a laugh.

"Funny, Sam."

"Seriously, though, give it a little more time before you decide."

"I'll think about it." Although she said she'd consider it, Lexia had all but made up her mind to end things. No sense in dragging it out. That would only result in her potentially getting hurt again.

When her cell buzzed with a text from Khalil a while later, Lexia contemplated not answering, but decided it was now or never.

Khalil: Hey, beautiful. Are you going to be busy tomorrow evening?

Lexia: Hey. Actually, yes. I have some things to prepare for. How's the studying coming?

Khalil: Not as fast as I'd like, but it's coming.

Lexia: I was thinking now since you're well on your way, you don't need my help.

Khalil: So, we're back to me being bad company again.

Lexia: No. I just don't think we should continue to see each other. I'm not looking for an involvement.

A few minutes passed before he replied: I understand and you're right. I have a lot on my plate right now and I need to concentrate on that. I'll see you around.

She held the phone against her chest as disappointment filled her. She didn't know what she expected him to say—maybe that he wanted them to continue seeing each other or something along those lines. But his response let her know that she had done the right thing.

Friday afternoon, Khalil sat with the design team at Gray Home Safety reviewing the first pieces of equipment that had been produced. He ran his hand over the curve of the two-pound dumbbell where the braille label would go. "It's perfect." They would be making them from one pound up to twenty pounds, initially. Currently, he had three members who had low vision, all women, so he'd wait to have the team produce the heavier weights until the women tried them out and Khalil could determine their effectiveness. They discussed the production schedule and other details and, as the meeting ended, Brandon entered. He nodded and focused his attention on the papers the production manager handed him.

Once everyone cleared the room, Brandon propped a hip on the table. "How's it going?"

Khalil briefed him on the particulars. "They did a great job. I think the label will fit nicely."

"Good. I see you've removed the wrist brace."

He flexed his wrist and fingers. "That thing was driving me crazy. It made my hand hurt worse."

"What about everything else?"

"It is what it is." Almost three weeks had passed and still not one sound in either ear.

Brandon dropped down into the chair next to Khalil. "Have you given any more thought into checking out some of the resources Dr. Moyer gave you?"

"No." He hadn't looked at them once after leaving the office. "But Lexia let me borrow her book on sign language."

"Lexia? You're seeing her?"

"Not seeing her really. Just hanging out."

Brandon threw his head back and laughed.

Khalil frowned. "What's so funny?"

"You. I warned you about her that first day. I'm telling you, if you keep 'hanging out'—" he made quote marks in the air "—you're going to end up in the same spot as Siobhan, Morgan and me. And don't try to lie about not having feelings for her."

"She's a beautiful woman. Of course I'd be attracted to her. That doesn't mean I'm ready to propose."

"If memory served me correctly, you've already done that. All you need to do is set the date. I'm sure Mom would love that."

Khalil leaned back in the leather chair and scrubbed a hand down his face. He'd forgotten about the teasing proposal he'd made to Lexia. And his mother. She'd taken an instant liking to Lexia, as evidenced by her extending an invitation to the family dinner. He didn't even want to think about what would have happened if she'd come. Siobhan seemed to like her, as well, and he had no doubts that the rest of his family would feel the same. But after their conversation two days ago, it was a moot point. Lexia had asked for some space and he'd given it.

"Since you're dating Lexia, won't it be a little tricky for you to escort that model to the fund-raiser. When is it again?"

"We're not dating. It's in three weeks and I won't be escorting Rosalyn. Apparently, my being deaf excludes me as a candidate," he said sarcastically.

"Are you serious?"

"Very."

"I thought you were one of the people who started the thing in the first place. Are you still going?"

"I don't know." What if a lot more people felt the same way? The isolation he'd experienced at dinner with his family would be magnified a hundredfold. Khalil wasn't sure he wanted to spend money flying across the country just to be an outcast. He could think of other ways to spend his time. "But I promised the kids I'd be there." He mentored a group of four teens, made sure they kept up with their studies and made sure they didn't fall into some of the pitfalls, like drugs, sex and hanging with the wrong crowds, that could ruin their lives. Khalil had been fortunate that his parents, Siobhan and Brandon kept his feet solidly on the ground.

"I don't think Faith and I have anything planned for that weekend. If you want us to go with you, let me know."

"Thanks." Though they sometimes didn't see eye to eye, Khalil appreciated his older brother. He chuckled inwardly. Brandon took being the older brother to the nth degree sometimes and Khalil knew Brandon would punch out the first person who said something disrespectful.

"Then again, you could always take Lexia."

"Didn't we just have this conversation? It's not that kind of relationship." It wasn't a relationship at all. He had no intentions of telling Brandon that Lexia had given him the boot. Khalil would never live it down, considering it had never happened before.

"Yeah, we had it, but I've been where you are. I said the same thing. Remember? And, as I recall, you weren't very sympathetic." He pushed to his feet. "And I like Lexia." He shook his head. "I still can't believe the way she walked into that hospital room and checked your hand and mouth, then told you to eat."

Neither could Khalil. Then again, she didn't have any problems holding her own with him. The only time she'd seemed vulnerable was when he'd blown up at her. Uneasiness settled in his chest with the thought. He never wanted to see tears in her eyes again, especially ones he had put there. He sighed inwardly. None of this mattered anymore. He needed to stop thinking about her and move on.

"That was pure comedy." Brandon chuckled. "So much for there not being a woman alive who can make you give up your single status. My money is on Lexia."

He leveled Brandon with a lethal glare. "Don't you have a company to run? I thought you were leaving."

Brandon smiled and held up his hands in mock surrender. "I'll let you off the hook for the time being, but I remember how you did me. And you know what they say about payback. Don't forget to let me know about the fundraiser. I can make it a date weekend with my wife."

"I can't believe you're standing here talking about your *wife*. What happened to that bachelor-for-life stance?"

"Love happened." He pivoted on his heel and walked out.

Love? Khalil didn't see himself making the same mistake twice. He'd never told anyone in his family about the woman he'd come close to marrying. The woman who had cost him the worst thirty-six hours of his life, hours he would never get back. Images of the cold, damp space, along with the never forgotten stench filled his mind. He bowed his head and willed the sensations to leave him. Now there was Lexia. But for him, there was no such thing as love.

Chapter 12

Lexia hadn't talked to Khalil since their conversation a week ago. She figured if she created some distance between them, she wouldn't want him so much, but she still couldn't get him off her mind. He hadn't reached out to her, either. But why would he when she had all but told him she wasn't interested anymore? Was he still practicing sign language or had he gone back to the frustrated man who shut everyone out?

"Stop thinking about him," she muttered. She had a ton of things to do to get ready for her cooking demonstration on Saturday and only two days to manage it all. The whistling of the tea kettle drew her out of her thoughts. She poured water over the bag and let it steep before adding a little sugar.

Lexia took her cup and went to sit on her three-by-five-foot balcony, which in no way compared to either of the large areas at Khalil's place. She had room for a chair and small table, and not much else. And, unlike the stunning views of the sky and water, all she could see from her second-floor unit was a tree and more condos. Instantly, her mind conjured up images of Khalil holding her as they watched the sunset. The peace and contentment she had experienced in his arms gave her pause and was one more reason she had to stay away from him. He made her long for the closeness in an intimate relationship again. Lexia groaned.

She set the cup aside and picked up the notepad she had left on the table earlier with the list of items she needed to shop for later to make sure she hadn't forgotten anything. Tomorrow she planned to leave work early so she would have plenty of time to prep her meal. This was the second year in a row Lexia had participated in the cooking festival held at one of the area's parks that benefited a local homeless shelter. During the two-day weekend affair, consumers would have the opportunity to sample a variety of foods prepared by the contributing chefs. The lesser, unknown chefs, like Lexia, occupied the earlier times. Big-name chefs, who prepared a full three-course meal while patrons sat at tables positioned around the makeshift kitchens, filled the evening slots. She had been fortunate enough to secure a Saturday noon slot, perfect for the lunch crowd and which left her time to recuperate before having to go back to work on Monday.

After double-checking her list, Lexia finished her tea and left to shop. She spent the remainder of the evening doing as much preparation as she could and labeling her containers.

The next morning Lexia could barely keep her eyes open. She had gone to bed after midnight and was up and at the café by five.

"You keep nodding off like that, you're liable to miss an ingredient in that recipe."

Stifling a yawn, she glanced over at Mr. Willis. "I'm not nodding off."

Mr. Willis let out a short bark of laughter. "No? So what is it that they're calling it these days when your eyes drift closed and your head falls forward?"

A smile peeped out. "All right, fine. I'm nodding off. I only got about four hours of sleep last night."

He shook his head and wagged a finger her way. "I told you to take off the whole day. Folks would be okay if they didn't get that coffee cake for one day. Just hardheaded. Don't come looking for me when you bang your head against the counter because you fell asleep," he fussed.

Lexia laughed. "I'll be fine. I plan to take a nap as soon

as I get home before I get started. Are you coming tomorrow?"

"Of course. You know I have to support my girl. This is a good cause...and the food ain't bad, either."

She agreed. Seeing what Cameron went through and the increasing number of homeless and hopeless people inspired her to do more than just contribute a few dollars here and there. She wanted to do something to impact their lives. She had some other ideas, but no money to get it done. So for now, they continued to be just dreams.

Lexia managed to get the coffee cakes into the oven without mishap and made herself a cup of English breakfast tea. Today she needed the caffeine.

Sam arrived half an hour later. "Morning, Lexi."

"Morning."

"You look exhausted. Long night?"

"Yep. Started prepping for tomorrow. I already got an earful from Mr. Willis about why I should have taken off the day and how hardheaded I am, so you can save your fussing. And I *will* be taking a nap after I leave."

Sam smiled and busied herself with starting the coffee and making sure the hot water container was filled. "How's Khalil doing?"

"I have no idea."

She spun around. "You did it, didn't you?"

"If you mean telling him we need to slow things down, yes. He obviously thought the same thing because he agreed and said he had a lot going on, so..."

Sam rolled her eyes. "Of course he'd say that. He probably doesn't want to be hurt, either. He hasn't even been in for his favorite snack and I saw him twice in the past week. I *knew* you sent that text. So you aren't going to check up on him to see how he's doing? Or find out whether his hearing has returned?"

Lexia had been tempted all week to send him a text to find out, but so far hadn't given in to the urge. "I'm sure I can find out from Brandon or Siobhan when they stop in for lunch."

Sam shook her head disapprovingly. "I don't know about you, girlfriend. I think he's a great guy."

So did she, and that was the bulk of her problem. In the short time she had known Khalil, she'd seen many facets of the man—charming, vulnerable, respectful, sensual, caring. It would be too easy for her to lose her heart to him. Hell, she was halfway there already, especially after seeing him interact with Anthony. He would have had to reveal his own hurts in order to reach the young man and Khalil hadn't hesitated. Elyse had told Lexia that Anthony was now actually participating in class.

"What are you going to do about the feelings you have for him?"

"I don't have feelings for him anymore. It was nothing more than a little lust."

"You are such a liar," Sam said, and pinned Lexia with a look, waiting.

"Fine, I don't know what to do. I thought by not seeing or talking to him, they would go away."

"But they're not."

"No." She sighed deeply. "I don't understand why. I've never had this problem before."

"That's because you never met anyone like Khalil."

No, she hadn't. How could she not fall for a guy who revealed his weaknesses to her without shame and who kissed her like he had perfected the art just to please her?

By Friday of the following week, Khalil couldn't take it any longer. He thought he could dismiss Lexia as easily as he'd done previous women, but nothing worked. Over the past ten days, he found himself thinking about her no matter the time of day. And at night, he'd had dreams so vivid and real he could feel the heat of her body against his and smell the soft citrusy fragrance she wore. He had awakened the last two mornings and reached for her, only to find an empty space. He knew she felt the same attraction he did. Her eyes and kiss told him. Something else had to be going on with her. And as soon as he finished his meeting with the construction supervisor at his new building, he was going over to the café to try to convince her to reconsider.

He refocused his attention on the blueprints laid out in front of him. The opening was still on schedule to open early June and the contractors were now working on the interior. Khalil walked around the spacious area, pleased with the progress. "It looks good, Dan."

"Thanks. I'll email you the specs with the changes you asked for by Monday."

"Appreciate it." They shook hands and Khalil headed out to his car. He settled behind the wheel and felt his phone vibrate in his pocket. His mother.

Hey, baby. Just wanted to check on you and make sure you're not overdoing it at work. And I KNOW you aren't in that gym lifting weights or doing any kind of workout.

Khalil had to laugh. His mother knew him well. He hadn't gone more than a few days without some kind of exercise since he hit sixteen and not working out was killing him. He thought about just doing a set or two of push-ups, but his wrist still couldn't hold him comfortably. And his one attempt at doing crunches two days ago had caused him so much pain he seriously wondered if he'd ever be able to work out again. Even planking for more than a few seconds was out of the question. He sent her a message back telling her he was fine and that he was only going to the gym to work, nothing more. Before he could pocket it, it buzzed again.

Alonzo: You might want to get over to the gym. Your boy has made a move.

Khalil: What do you mean? You caught him in the system?

Alonzo: That and more. I'll meet you there in 15 min.

Khalil's heart started pounding. More? What else was Logan doing? He started the car, threw the gear into first and sped out of the lot. He was so preoccupied with trying to figure out what Alonzo's cryptic message meant that he forgot about his driving apprehension.

He pulled into his spot twenty minutes later, hopped out of the car and froze with a shock of pain from the sudden movement. He groaned and slowed his pace.

Khalil snatched the door open, nodded to the staff and went directly to his office. He found Alonzo talking with Felicia in the hallway outside of Khalil's office. "Hey, Felicia. Alonzo."

She waved and ducked into her office.

He unlocked the door, gestured Alonzo in and closed the door. "What the hell is going on?"

Alonzo handed Khalil the iPad with video footage. "See for yourself."

Khalil's heart nearly stopped. Logan was jimmying the lock on Khalil's office, logging on to the computer and accessing at least ten members' profiles and debiting their accounts. Alonzo opened another file. Khalil stared grimly as he watched Logan remove some of the gym equipment and load it into his truck with the help of another man. "When was this?"

"Last night after closing."

"Call 911. Tell them they need to send the police and an ambulance because I'm about to kick Logan's ass." He opened the door with such force it hit the wall. He strode out of the office toward the elevator.

Felicia took one look at his face and jumped out of the way.

Alonzo caught up with Khalil at the elevator and the two men rode to the first floor.

When they exited, Alonzo placed a staying hand on Khalil's arm. "Man—"

He turned a blazing look on Alonzo that made the man remove his hand and take a step back. Khalil burst into Logan's office with Alonzo on his heels.

Logan jumped to his feet and divided a wary glance between the two men. "What's going on?"

He charged around the desk and, without a word, threw a solid left punch across Logan's jaw that knocked him out cold. A string of expletives erupted from Khalil's mouth as pain shot through his midsection. He took several shallow breaths, wrapped his right hand around his middle and braced his left hand on the desk, waiting for the pain to subside.

Alonzo, with a smile on his face, gestured to a chair.

Khalil lowered himself to the seat and leaned his head back. He would probably pay for that hit later, but the man deserved it.

Alonzo hauled Logan to his feet, tossed the semiconscious man into a chair and placed the cell on the desk in front of him.

It took everything in Khalil not to go around the desk again. "Be glad I only hit you once."

Logan rubbed his jaw. "I'm suing you!"

"Before or after I have you prosecuted for debiting the accounts of several members and stealing my gym equipment?" he countered. "Oh, and you're fired."

Logan's eyes went wide.

"That's what I thought. And please don't try to insult my intelligence and say you didn't do it. We have you on video. You will pay back every penny you stole from the members." Khalil had fronted the money and reimbursed their accounts, but he planned to get his money back. "Or I can send them all memos letting them know you're the one who broke into their accounts. I'm certain they'd want to file a class action suit. And my equipment…you have two minutes to tell me where the police can find it…and your friend."

"Police?"

He stared at him incredulously. "What did you think was going to happen?"

Alonzo pointed behind Khalil and mouthed, "Police."

Khalil stood to greet the officers and let Alonzo do most of the explaining after becoming frustrated with one of the officers, who kept talking without using the cell. Khalil had to ask the officer to repeat himself several times and point out that he couldn't understand without the technology.

Once Logan had been handcuffed and escorted off the property, Alonzo filled Khalil in on the information Logan had provided.

"Apparently, he was trying to open his own gym, but didn't have the money necessary to make the down payment. He also needed equipment, so instead of buying his own, he started taking a few pieces out of here—mostly free weights, some mats, exercise bands and medicine balls."

He cursed under his breath. "Did he tell them where my stuff is?"

"Yes. They're going to confiscate it all and you'll have to go down to identify what's yours. The police want you to bring whatever paperwork you have to show ownership."

"That shouldn't be too difficult since I keep everything." Most of the free weights he had designed himself and had the gym's logo engraved on them. The clock on the wall read one. He had planned to be at the café by now. If he left within the next ten minutes, he could make it before closing. "Thanks for everything, Alonzo."

"Anytime. Guess you'll need a new manager now."

Khalil groaned. He didn't even want to think about having to go through the interviewing process again. Hopefully, Felicia would agree to step into the position. He still had a little time to find someone for the new site. "I'm going to go talk to Felicia."

"I'll follow up with the police and let you know what I find out. I'll catch you later."

He stood in the office a moment longer, still in disbelief, then went back upstairs and knocked on Felicia's open door.

"Logan was the one?" she asked.

"Yeah. He was also stealing the equipment."

Felicia's mouth dropped. "This morning someone mentioned they couldn't find the twenty-pound dumbbells and I was going to ask you about it."

"Well, he'll be paying my money back and returning my stuff. Felicia, now that you're just about finished with your degree, would you consider taking the manager's position?"

"Are you sure?"

"Absolutely. I wanted you to have it when Jessie left, but you mentioned not wanting to pick up too many hours because of school."

A smile blossomed on her face. "Then, yes."

"Thanks and congratulations. That's one less thing I have to worry about. I'm taking off for a bit, but I'll be back later."

"Okay, and thanks, Khalil."

Khalil got to the café fifteen minutes before it closed. "Hey, Sam. Is Lexia in the back?"

Sam shook her head and scribbled on the order pad, "She left early to prepare for a cooking demonstration at the Project Food festival tomorrow."

"She's cooking?"

She nodded.

"Where is it?"

Sam hesitated, then pulled a flyer out of her pocket and handed it to him.

He scanned the sheet. The location was almost in his backyard and benefited a homeless shelter. Why hadn't he ever heard of the event? He memorized the website and handed it back.

She held up a hand and pushed it toward him.

"Do they have a schedule of when each chef will be cooking?"

"She'll be doing her demonstration at noon."

"I'll be there. Oh, and don't tell her I'm coming."

A smile curved Sam's lips. "Okay." Then she wrote something else. "But if you hurt my girl, I'm going to hurt you." She gave him a pointed look.

"I don't plan to hurt her."

She folded her arms and nodded.

"I'll see you later." He glanced down at the flyer once more and smiled. He couldn't wait to see Lexia's face.

Saturday, Khalil arrived at the festival an hour before Lexia's demonstration. Immediately, a sense of unease crept up his spine. Masses of festivalgoers passed by him, talking and laughing. His breathing increased and an overwhelming need to leave engulfed him. He stood off to the side where fewer people lingered for a few minutes to get his bearings. Even after almost a month, he still became anxious in crowds. Once in control, he wandered around the grounds and sampled a green smoothie, dried fruit and roasted eggplant Parmesan. He pulled out the map and searched the key to find where Lexia would be and started in that direction. He spotted her setting up her outdoor kitchen area that held counter space and what looked like a stove top. Not wanting her to see him yet, he took up a position far enough away to be out of her line of sight, but close enough to view her comfortably. She wore a chef's jacket and moved around the space efficiently and expertly.

Khalil had missed her more than he realized. She smiled and he felt a strange sensation in his belly. He kept telling himself he wasn't in the market for a relationship, but he wanted her nearness. He was confident the rest would work out. He noticed a small crowd of people drifting over to her station and taking seats. He waited another few minutes and walked over just as she began. Their eyes met and she froze. He smiled and gave her an imperceptible nod, which she returned and continued. Two minutes into the demonstration, he recognized that she, indeed, knew what she was doing. He couldn't get close enough to understand what she said, but she prepared some type of shrimp taco with the expertise of a seasoned chef.

When it ended, she and Sam passed out the tacos to those in the audience. The eager crowd jostled for position to get a sample. By the looks on their faces, it must taste good. Khalil waited until the last person left before approaching.

Lexia handed him a taco and he purposely allowed their

hands to touch. She withdrew hers quickly and her gaze flew to his.

Still holding her eyes, Khalil bit into the warm taco. An involuntary groan slipped out. "This is really good."

She smiled up at him.

He polished it off in two more bites. He moved closer to her. "Can we talk when you're done here?"

Lexia paused, biting on her bottom lip, and he pushed down the longing to kiss her. Finally she nodded.

He told her where he'd be waiting and got out of her way. The faster she got done, the sooner she'd be in his arms.

Chapter 13

Lexia knew that Khalil was watching her every move. She'd almost fallen off the small stand when she looked up and saw him in the back of the audience. How had he found out about the festival? She searched her mind and tried to recall whether she had mentioned it to him, but didn't think she had. That left only one person. Sam.

"Sam, did you tell Khalil about today?"

Without looking up from packing away the utensils, Sam said, "Yep. He came to the café yesterday asking for you. He seemed so pitiful when he found out you weren't there. I couldn't help myself. Go ahead and admit it. You know you're glad to see him."

She wasn't going to admit anything, least of all the fact that the first thing she wanted to do when she saw him was throw her arms around him and kiss him with everything within her. Lexia busied herself with cleaning the stove top and grill for the next chef. Afterward, they loaded everything on the provided cart and Khalil helped wheel it out to her car.

"I'm going to check out a few of the vendors," Sam said. "I'll see you on Monday. Get some rest. You've earned it."

"Thanks for all your help."

She hugged Lexia. "Have fun and be nice."

She ignored her friend. "Bye."

"Bye, Khalil." Sam waved.

When they were alone, Khalil grasped Lexia's hand and entwined their fingers. "Can we find a spot that's less crowded?"

Lexia led him over to the far side of the grounds away from the vendors and found a bench. For the first minutes, they just sat with his arm wrapped around her and her head on his shoulder.

He tilted her chin. "I don't know what I was thinking agreeing to not see you anymore. I missed you, Lexia." He lowered his head and placed a soft kiss against her lips. "Why did you back away? Was it something I did?"

"No."

"Then why?"

She took out her cell. "You're a special man and I really like you, but I don't want to get caught up in another relationship with the potential to get my heart broken. Been there, done that with my ex-husband. I'm finally putting the pieces of my life back together and I like the peace. That's why I named the café Oasis. It's my haven, my place of refuge."

He sat stunned by her revelation. *Married?* "How long were you married?" She held up two fingers. "He cheated?"

"And took the one thing I loved. The diner we purchased. I had been going there since I was a teen and when the owner passed away suddenly, my ex knew I wanted it and helped me finance it. In the end, he had a better lawyer. I didn't care about the house, the cars, the money, just my diner. And he stole it."

Lexia swiped at the tears gathered in her eyes. She thought she'd finished crying.

Khalil gently pushed her hand aside and kissed her tears. "I'm sorry, sweetheart. He can't hurt you anymore. And if he ever shows up, he'll have to go through me." He tightened his arm around her.

She glanced up at him. The sincerity in his features and protective gesture gave her pause. She hadn't expected him to say something like that—as if they were a couple. "What are we doing here, Khalil?"

"We're sitting on a bench talking."

She slanted him a look. "You know what I mean."

He blew out a long breath. "I'm not sure…exactly. I just know I like spending time with you. I like talking to you, touching you, kissing you…" He captured her mouth in a brief but scorching kiss. "Especially kissing you." He stared at her a moment. "You are so very different in a good way and I can't seem to stop wanting you."

Just like that, she fell a little harder. They sat awhile longer, then wandered around to see some of the other demonstrations. An hour later, he walked her out to her car.

"What are you doing tomorrow?"

"Just relaxing. Why?"

"I owe you a couple of training sessions and I thought we could start."

Lexia remembered him saying that, but figured he had been kidding around. "You were serious?"

Khalil chuckled. "Of course."

"Well…um…don't you think that might be too strenuous for you? I don't want you to hurt yourself."

"I'm not the one who'll be working out, you will."

She hadn't been inside a gym in a good five or six years and, even then, she'd only done a couple of exercise classes, never the weights. She could just imagine the crazy looks she'd get. "I haven't worked out in a long time."

"The gym is closed on Sundays, so there'll be no one there but us."

That's a relief. "Okay, but not too early because I want to sleep in."

He smiled. "How about three? That way you can sleep in and run any errands. Oh, and I'm coming to pick you up."

Lexia rolled her eyes. "This isn't a date, Khalil."

"Doesn't matter."

They engaged in a staredown until she sighed in surrender. "Fine. Like I can't drive myself," she muttered, and unlocked her car.

"I know you said something smart, but like I said, it doesn't matter." Khalil held the door open, bent and placed a kiss on her lips. "Let me know when you get home."

"I will." As she drove off, Lexia tried to contemplate a way to get out of that workout. The mere thought of his heat surrounding her while demonstrating some exercise technique aroused her. More than aroused her.

Khalil let him and Lexia into the gym Sunday afternoon and locked the door behind them. "Stay right here while I turn on some lights." With the blinds closed, it was so dark, he could barely see and he didn't want her to trip over anything. But he knew the place like the back of his hand, so he didn't have a problem navigating by instinct. He pressed a wall switch and a small section of lights came on, providing enough illumination for them to accomplish their task, but not enough for anyone to see from outside.

Lexia came to where he stood. "I've never lifted weights before."

"I told you I'd show you a few exercises to do that don't require a lot of equipment." He held up the large bag in his hand. From it, he withdrew a yoga mat, an eight-inch bouncing ball, a length of light resistance exercise band and a resistance strap with handles that could be attached to any door. This would be his first training session since the accident and, if it went well, he would start pulling his clients back.

"All that is supposed to be for a whole body workout?"

Khalil met Lexia's skeptical gaze. "Yep. And you can take all this home with you." He rolled out the mat. "We'll start with some stretches to warm up your muscles."

She came and sat on the mat. "As long as it's been since I've worked out, the stretches might be all I can handle."

He shook his head. "You'll be fine." He took her through a series of movements. Each time he touched her, he struggled to maintain a professional edge. It didn't help that she had worn a fitted sleeveless top and leggings that outlined every curve and he was tempted to reacquaint himself with the feel of her smooth skin.

Lexia finished the last one and sat up. "That wasn't so bad. What's next?"

Khalil came to his feet with the resistance band. "Upper body exercises. This one is for the chest and back." He grasped the band on either end, held his arms straight out in front of him at ninety degrees and pulled until his arms were out to his side. He felt a slight twinge of pain, but nothing like it had been. He did one more repetition and handed it to Lexia. "Let's start with two sets of fifteen, resting for thirty seconds between each set."

"Okay." She finished the first exercise with ease, but by the time she got to the third one, he could see her arms trembling.

"Only six more. You can do it. Come on, baby."

Lexia finished and dropped her arms down to her side. "I can't do this. My arms feel like lead."

"Yes you can. This is only your first session. Your arms can rest while we do a few for the lower body." Khalil led her over to a bar mounted on the wall. "At home you can use the back of a chair to hold on to for squats. Don't go down too far or let your knees go beyond your toes. I want you to concentrate on your form like this." He did a set of fifteen with her. His mother would have a heart attack if she found out, but it felt good to do something other than lie around all day. Next he had her lie on the mat. He placed the ball between her bent knees. "This will work your inner thighs. I want you to squeeze, hold for three seconds and release. Three sets of twenty."

She flopped down on the mat. "Okay. That's easier than those squats. By the time we finish, I'd better be able to win the Miss Fitness contest."

Khalil laughed. "I'll see what I can do." Three reps into the first set, he began to think this wasn't a good idea. Watching her squeeze the ball sent visions of her knees pressing against him as he thrust deep inside her. Blood rushed to his groin and he closed his eyes briefly to force the images away. Lexia touched his hand. He flinched and his eyes popped open.

Lexia came up on her knees. "Are you hurting? I thought you hurt your right hand."

"I'm fine and I did. My hand is sore from knocking the hell out of my manager yesterday. I'll tell you about it after we're done. I don't want your muscles to get cold." Her concerned gaze searched his face, seemingly to gauge if he was being truthful. "I promise I'm okay. Lie back down and keep your knees bent."

She nodded and resumed her previous position.

Khalil tied the resistance band around her knees. He ran his hand up the outside of her thighs. "This is for your outer thighs." He pulled her knees apart, stretching the band. "Three sets of twenty, holding for three seconds." Once again, he had to look away. The sight of her slightly spread legs conjured up memories of the way she had clamped down on his hand as he pleasured her. He grew harder and harder. By the end of her first set, he couldn't take it anymore. Khalil reached over and untied the band.

Lexia braced herself on an elbow. "What are you doing? That was only one set. I thought you said three. I'm not finished."

"No, you aren't. But we're going to have to finish it in a

different way." Khalil got up on all fours and moved until he was over her. "Do you know how hard it is for me to sit here and watch you, when all I want to do is make love to you? Let me show you how much, baby."

She lifted her hand and signed, *yes*.

He lowered his head and captured her mouth in a slow, drugging kiss. He'd wanted her from the first time they met. He had planned for their first time to be in a bed, but there was no way he'd make the ten-minute drive to her house. "We really should be doing this in a bed, but I can't wait, sweetheart. I promise to make it up to you next time." He came to his knees, bringing her into a sitting position and removed her top and blue sports bra. He kissed her back down on the mat and trailed kisses over her neck, chest and breasts. He used his tongue to tease and suck, first one nipple, then the other. Khalil kissed his way down her belly, hooked his thumbs in the waistband of her leggings and slid them, along with her panties, down and off. He tossed them aside and continued his quest. His lips grazed her center, inner thighs and behind her knees. She arched and writhed, arousing him further. He took another slow tour back up her body, pausing to shed his own clothes and don a condom. He lowered himself on her and shuddered as their warm, naked flesh came together.

Lexia grasped his head and pulled him down for a kiss that left him gasping for breath. "What are you waiting for?" she mouthed.

"For you to invite me in."

She smiled, reached between them, grabbed his shaft and guided him inside her.

It was all the invitation he needed. Her tight walls clenched him and he gritted his teeth to keep from losing control. "You ready to finish your workout?"

She nodded.

"Good. I know we already worked your inner thighs, but one more set won't hurt. Squeeze your knees against me just like you did with the ball." He punctuated each press with a slow, deep thrust, pulling out to the tip each time. They both trembled. He kept up the measured pace and watched the play of passion across her features.

Her nails dug into the flesh of his back and she arched higher to take him deeper.

Khalil fused his mouth with hers and she twirled her tongue around his, provocatively and sensually. He groaned. "Now," he said as he shifted until his thighs were on the outside of hers, "you have two more sets to work these." His hands feathered down her hips to her knees.

Lexia's mouth opened with a perfect O and her eyes drifted closed. In this position, he grazed her clit with every stroke.

The pressure of her holding him so snugly made him increase the tempo, delving deeper into her with each rhythmic push and she matched his fluid movements. Khalil gripped her hips and ground his body into hers. Her body began to shake and he buried his face in her throat, needing to feel the vibration of her voice when she came. As spasms racked her body, it triggered his own release and the climax shot through him with a force that left him weak and panting. He groaned and called her name. Closing his eyes, he collapsed and shifted his body so as not to put all his weight on her. For weeks he had imagined what it would be like when they finally made love, but the real thing had surpassed his most erotic fantasies. Lexia tapped him on the shoulder and he lifted his head.

"I think we ruined this mat. I've never had a workout quite like this."

Khalil leaned over to read what she'd said and laughed. "I should hope not. And neither have I." He could tell his answer pleased her. He kissed her, slowly got to his feet and helped her up. "Come on. Let's go shower." He was going to do his best to let her shower alone, but a vision of him taking her against the shower wall surfaced in his mind and he knew it was a long shot.

They gathered up their clothes and Lexia followed Khalil upstairs to what she realized was his office. His fluid gait had her mesmerized and she could now answer definitively that, yes, his firm, muscled butt was as tight as it looked. She couldn't believe she'd just had sex in a gym. Her body still tingled and pulsed and all she could think of was doing it again. She glanced around the functional space that held a large desk with a computer and several neatly stacked piles of folders, a couple of file cabinets and a bookshelf.

Khalil unlocked another door behind the desk that led to a private bathroom, complete with an oversize shower. He got towels from a built-in shelf and turned on the water. "You can go first, or…" He slid an arm around her waist and nuzzled her neck. "Or we can shower together to save time." He slanted his mouth over hers in a heated kiss, while his hands roamed and caressed her body.

Lexia reached down, grasped his hard shaft and backed him toward the open shower door. She hoped he had more condoms.

He reversed their positions and let her go first. "Be right back." Moments later, he stepped in behind her, condom in place, as well as earplugs.

Before she could say anything, he cupped one breast in his hand, dipped his head and latched on to her nipple. He traced a path down the front of her body with his other hand and pushed two fingers into her pulsing core. She gasped sharply and braced her hands on the shower wall to steady herself. Her head fell back as a whirlwind of sensations whipped through her. Khalil withdrew his fingers, fisted his hands in her hair and crushed his mouth against hers in an urgent kiss. Without breaking the seal of their mouths, he lifted her with one arm and entered her with one long stroke. He placed her against the cool tile, gripped her hips in his hands and started a driving rhythm that had her on the verge of another orgasm almost immediately.

"Can you feel what you do to me? Feel how much I want you?"

Yes, she could. She felt every inch of his thick hardness surging in and out of her. Lexia wrapped her legs around his waist, tilted her hips and contracted her feminine muscles.

Khalil cursed. "Don't do that," he said through clenched teeth.

She gave him a sultry smile and did it again.

"Oh, so you want to play, huh?" He lowered her to her feet, spun her around, bent her forward and entered her from behind.

Lexia thought she would faint from all the pleasure he was giving her. He pounded inside of her until she convulsed in a blinding climax and screamed his name. Her knees buckled and, had he not tightened his grip on her waist, she would have slid to the floor.

Khalil went rigid, then shuddered uncontrollably, yelling out her name as he came. He placed one hand on the wall above her head and continued to hold her. He pulled out, turned her in his arms and kissed her tenderly. "We'd better wash up for real this time. I think the hot water will be gone in a minute."

The water had started to cool, but he adjusted the knob and it warmed a little more. They washed each other, dried off and dressed without speaking. No words were needed. Lexia tried to do something with her hair and remembered that he had put his hands in her hair after touching her. She groaned inwardly. So, instead of the relaxing evening she had planned, she would have to spend three hours washing her hair.

Downstairs, he placed all of her equipment in the bag. He rolled up the mat and grinned. "I guess I owe you another one."

She picked up her cell from the floor where she had left it and placed her hand on her hip. "That's not all you owe me."

He looked up from his phone and frowned. "What did I do?"

"My hair. You do remember having your hands all in it after…you know… Anyway, now I'm going to have to spend the next three hours washing and styling it."

Khalil's eyes widened. "*Three hours?* Why does it take so long?"

"Well, let's see, I have to part it in about seven or eight sections, precondition it and comb through each section—*separately*—gently with a wide-tooth comb to detangle and get rid of shed hair. Then I have to shampoo it, one section at a time to keep it from getting tangled." She chuckled at the stunned look on his face and continued. "After which, I apply a deep conditioner, cover it with a plastic cap and sit under the dryer for thirty minutes." His mouth fell open. "Oh, I'm not done yet. Then I rinse out the conditioner, dry it with a cotton T-shirt, apply a leave-in conditioner, styling crème and coconut oil to seal in the moisture and braid it."

"I guess I do owe you." He angled his head thoughtfully. "I tell you what, if you make me a couple of those tacos from yesterday, I'll help you with your hair."

Lexia stared in disbelief. He was offering to help do her hair? Her ex-husband had never done that. Whenever she washed her hair, he complained about how long it took, how much water she used, how many different products lined the counter and any other thing he could think of.

He'd even tried to get her to go back to relaxers. But Khalil hadn't hesitated to offer his assistance.

"So do we have a deal?"

"Yes. Do you promise to behave yourself?"

"I have no idea what you're talking about," he said with mock innocence.

She raised an eyebrow and waited.

"I promise to be on my best behavior."

"Good." Now if only she could promise herself the same thing.

Chapter 14

Khalil combed out the last section of Lexia's hair and braided it. She had been correct about how much time it would take, but he found himself enjoying the process. Her hair always smelled good—fruity with a hint of vanilla—and he wondered what she put in it. Now he knew. She sat between his legs on a pillow placed on the floor, while he sat on the sofa. The last time he'd been here, he'd only stayed a moment, so hadn't gotten a good look at her condo. The walls had been painted with the standard cream color, but the added shades of purple gave the room a warm, homey feeling.

Lexia reached up and patted her hair, then turned to face him. She reached for her cell. "You did a great job. I may have to ask you to help me every time." She leaned up to kiss him. "How did you get so good at this?"

Khalil glanced down at his cell on the sofa. "My younger sister, Morgan, was a bona fide tomboy and she sprained her wrist at least four times a year."

She laughed. "Wow. What was she doing?"

"Most often, it was from playing football."

"Football?"

"Yep. She still plays it whenever she can."

"That's something. What does she do?"

Khalil smiled. "She's a sports agent...and she's married to her first client, Omar Drummond." Omar and Khalil's younger brother, Malcolm, played professional football on the local team—the LA Cobras.

Lexia's eyes lit up. "I know who he is. I remember reading about him having a female agent and some drama with his former agent. *That's* your sister?"

He nodded.

"How cool."

"Do you like football?"

"I do and, yes, the Cobras are my favorite team." She made a move to stand and accidently hit his hand. When he winced, she said, "Sorry. You were going to tell me about what happened." She sat next to him on the sofa and tucked one leg under her body.

"I found out the manager was double and triple charging some of the gym's members. That's what the call was about that I took the day of the explosion. My assistant manager had busted him going into my office." He told her about the cameras and how they caught him on the computer and stealing the equipment.

"So, you hit him."

"Knocked him out cold." Just the thought made him want to find Logan and hit him again.

"I can't blame you. I might've done the same thing."

Khalil wanted to ask about her ex, but didn't. Had she hit him? With her spunk, he could see her throwing a punch or two.

"I'm assuming you fired him."

"As soon as he regained consciousness."

Lexia fell back on the sofa and her shoulders shook with laughter. When she calmed herself, she asked, "So, what are you going to do?"

"I promoted the assistant manager, but that still leaves me short for the new gym opening in a couple of months."

"What kind of person are you looking for?"

"Someone who's honest and trustworthy, for starters." His gut had told him something was off about Logan, but the man had glowing references, so Khalil had ignored that voice. Never again. "I need a person who has some business and finance background and ideally, experience in fitness. Why, do you know someone?"

"Actually I do. Cameron really needs a job to get back on his feet."

Khalil's first response was no way, but he'd made assumptions about her friend the last time that were wrong. He now knew what it was like to be judged without having all the facts, so he kept his mouth shut. It also made him remember that he hadn't decided whether or not to attend the fund-raiser next weekend. "What kind of job did Cameron have before?"

"He was in management at one of the financial companies in the same building as your family's company."

"Really? Do you know where he's staying?"

"Right now, he's staying in a room I fixed up in the back of the café, but he's been searching for an apartment."

He didn't know how he felt about the man staying so close, but didn't speak to that, either. "I'll come by the café next week to talk to him." It couldn't hurt. "Would you like to go with me to a fund-raiser for youth models next weekend?" The words were out of his mouth before his brain registered them.

"I don't have any plans as yet. I thought you didn't model anymore."

"I don't, but I support this cause because it offers scholarships to the youth to encourage them to stay in school, teaches them about budgeting and saving, and provides money to help offset travel expenses for their families." Khalil left out the role he played.

"That's a great cause. I'd like to do something similar for the homeless community. After seeing what Cameron went through and listening to some of the stories he's shared, I want to make an impact."

He and his family always tried to find ways to give back and this sounded like a great idea. "Let me know what you plan to do and I'll help in any way I can."

"Thanks. So, about the fund-raiser, this is one of those high-priced, fancy shindigs, right?"

"It is."

"Okay, you've got a date." She wiggled her eyebrows. "All I need is an excuse to go shopping."

He read what she'd said and laughed until his chest hurt. Coupled with the strenuous workout he'd had earlier, he figured he would be in for a long night of aches. Lexia placed her hand softly against his chest and a strange sensation spread across the spot. *What was that?* His laughter faded.

"Are you okay? Maybe we shouldn't have… I'm sorry. I forgot you were still healing."

Khalil brought her hand to his lips. "I'll probably be sore tomorrow, but what we shared makes it all worth it." Lexia stared at him with a longing that had him contemplating one more round. But he didn't want to push it. And he had no more condoms. "So, I'll make the flight reservations when I get home." He already had a suite booked at the hotel.

Lexia sat up straight. "Flight? What do you mean flight? It's not in LA?"

He shook his head slowly. "New York." The look on her face was priceless and had him cracking up all over again. "Sweetheart, I need you to go easy on me. All this laughing is killing me."

"Why didn't you tell me it was in New York?"

"I just did." And Khalil couldn't wait to have the entire weekend with her. "We'll leave on Friday after you get off work. The event is on Saturday and we'll fly back sometime Sunday."

She expression turned serious. "Do they know about…?"

"Yeah. Originally, I was supposed to help a friend by escorting one of his newer clients, but he sent me a text canceling."

Anger clouded her features. "You have got to be kidding me? What does you not being able to hear have to do with anything? That's okay. We're going to walk into that room and—"

Khalil glanced up from his phone when she stopped. Knowing what he did about her and guessing by the way the letters flew across his screen, he imagined she was on a rant much like the one when she had called him arrogant and judgmental. He signed, *thank you*.

Lexia stopped. "You've been practicing."

He fingerspelled, *I have*. He was still very slow, but could remember most of the letters and a couple of the basic signs.

She smiled and twisted her hands back and forth in the air.

He returned her smile and checked the time. "I'd better go." As much as he didn't want to, he had to leave. They both had work in the morning and he had an appointment with Dr. Moyer, one he wasn't looking forward to since there had been no change in a month's time. "Walk me to the door." At the door, he took in her attire—the skimpy shorts and tank top she'd changed into—and braided hair. He fingered a braid. "I might need to stop by the café tomorrow so I can see my handiwork."

"Should I save you a piece of coffee cake?"

"Absolutely." Khalil bent and placed a brief kiss on her lips. If he did anything more, he most likely wouldn't leave until morning.

Lexia smiled and waved.

His gaze roamed over her once more and he left. He smiled. No woman he had dated would have ever let him see her like that, and certainly wouldn't have approved of him helping to wash her hair. None of them had piqued his interest for long, and maybe that was the other reason he'd pushed dating to the back burner. But, as he'd told Lexia, she was different in a good way. Too good because she was getting to him.

Friday, Lexia rushed around the café making sure the tabletops were clean and all the salt, pepper and sugar containers were full after the morning crowd had thinned. Only three customers remained for the time being. She and Khalil agreed that picking her up from here would save time since he would already be in the building for a meeting.

She glanced up when Cam came in. He had on a navy suit and reminded her of better times for him. "How did the interview go?"

Cam shrugged. "I didn't get a good feeling. This is the third one this week. First I'm overqualified, then it's not enough. And because I was out of work for over a year and can't account for that time..." He scrubbed a hand down his face.

"Hang in there. You've only been at it for a week and I'm sure something will come up soon." She hadn't mentioned what Khalil had said about possibly talking to Cam because she didn't want to give Cam any false hope if Khalil already had someone in mind.

"Thanks, Lexi. What do you need me to do in here?"

"I'm pretty much done with the tables, except for the ones that are occupied and Sam and Jayla already wrapped the utensils in napkins. The only thing left is getting ready for the next wave of customers."

He surveyed the room. "I'll help Sam and Jayla. Aren't you leaving early?"

"Probably around eleven thirty. Our flight is at two and you know LAX is a nightmare."

Cam folded his arms across his wide chest. "He treating you right?"

"Yes, Cam," Lexia said with exasperation. "And you can stop glaring at him every time he comes in."

He chuckled. "Hey, that's not what you said the last time."

"The last time was different." Cameron had been ready to dismember Desmond when he found out what the man had done. It had taken Jan and Lexia more than an hour to convince Cam that Desmond wasn't worth it. "Anyway…" She trailed off when her eyes locked with Khalil's as he came toward the café entrance.

Cam laughed. "Girl, you've got it bad. I sure hope it works out."

Lexia rolled her eyes, but was smiling. "Hush." She walked over to meet Khalil. "Hey."

Khalil placed a kiss on her temple. "Hey, baby. I know I'm a little early, but I wanted to talk to your friend."

"Okay."

He fingered a wavy strand. "I think I did a good job."

"Yes, you did." Images of him trailing kisses on her shoulders and neck as he helped her wash and condition her hair flashed in her mind. Lexia met his eyes and the slow grin appearing on his face let her know he was remembering, as well. She turned back to where Cameron still stood and beckoned him over and made introductions. "Cam, Khalil wants to talk to you." She handed Cam her phone. "You can use my phone to talk and he'll be able to read it on his." The technology hadn't been around when Elyse had lost her hearing, so Lexia and Jan had relied on writing notes and sign language. She pointed to a table on the far side of the room. "You can use that booth."

Cameron divided a speculative gaze between Lexia and Khalil, and then followed Khalil over.

Lexia sent up a silent prayer that the impromptu interview would go well. She noticed that the three people occupying the table were at the counter. She cleared the table and took the dishes to the kitchen.

Sam followed her a moment later. "Is Cameron grilling Khalil?"

"No. I think Khalil is talking to him about working as the manager in his new gym."

"*Seriously?* I thought he had a manager."

"He did until Saturday." She shared what Khalil had told her. "He said he knocked him out."

"I would've knocked the hell out of him, too. I can't believe he was taking equipment." She shook her head. "I don't know what's wrong with people today. Just crazy." Sam propped a hip against the sink. "So, are you ready for your weekend?"

"I guess. From what Khalil said, many of the people attending are connected to the modeling and entertainment business. I hope they're not like the ones on those reality TV shows."

"Well, if they are, I know you won't have any problems putting them in their place. But that's not what I mean. I'm talking about you being in a hotel room with that gorgeous man for two nights. It's been a month since his accident and he looks like he's healing nicely. Are you ready for what's going to happen?"

More like what's already *happened.* Lexia busied herself with scraping food off the plates and didn't comment.

Sam took the plate and observed Lexia. "Did you…?" She clapped a hand over her mouth. "You *did.*" She put the plate in the sink, grabbed Lexia's hand and nearly dragged her down the short hallway to Lexia's office. She closed the door and folded her arms. "Spill it."

Lexia dropped down in her chair. "Yeah, we did."

A smile played around the corners of Sam's mouth. "See, now aren't you glad I told him about the cooking show? Did he take you back to his house after I left you two? What does it look like?"

"We didn't go to his house afterward. I went to my place and he went to his...and he doesn't have a house, he has a condo. A *penthouse* condo. The views are to die for— the marina and ocean from the kitchen, living room and his bedroom. There's one wall that's made up of windows and—" She groaned inwardly. She hadn't meant to say all that.

"If you didn't go to his house on Saturday..."

"I went to visit him a couple of weeks ago. He asked me to help him learn sign language."

Her mouth dropped. "You slept with him two weeks ago and didn't tell me?"

She threw up her hands. "No, Sam. I did not. We practiced a few letters and I had planned to leave, but we ended up watching a movie and he cooked."

Sam's brows knit in puzzlement. "Okay. I'm confused."

"It happened last weekend...at his gym," she mumbled.

"Oh my. That must have been some workout." A wide grin spread across her lips.

"Shut up. I don't know what happened. One minute he was showing me some exercises, the next we were naked and...you know."

"And?"

"And what?"

"Girl, can the man bring it or what?"

Every detail of their encounter had replayed in her mind all last night with vivid clarity. She didn't think she would ever be able to do those exercises again without thinking about what happened. Even now, the memory of his thighs surrounding hers as he thrust deeply when he'd asked her to push against him made her core pulse.

"Lexia!" Sam snapped her fingers in Lexia's face.

She jumped. "What?"

"I asked you a question, but I already know the answer. Just looking at the way he moves says he can more than bring it."

"And he did," Lexia confessed.

A knock sounded on the door and Sam reached behind her to open it. She stepped aside so Khalil could enter. Behind his back, she mouthed, "You go, girl," and exited.

Khalil handed Lexia her phone. "So what did Sam say behind my back?"

She went still. "What makes you think she said anything?"

"I could feel the air from her voice."

She burst out laughing. Sam was only a few inches shorter than Khalil and she was close to his shoulder. "Are you ready? How did it go with Cam?"

"So, you're not going to answer my question?"

"It was nothing. Well?"

Khalil paused a beat. "Cameron is pretty impressive on the financial and management side, but he's never done anything in the fitness field. I have three more interviews to do next week before I decide. He seems like a nice guy."

"He is." She wanted to plead Cameron's case, but knew it wouldn't be fair to ask Khalil to hire him any more than it would be for Khalil to ask her to hire someone who lacked some of the experience she was seeking.

"He also shared some of the same things you did about helping the homeless community. I told him we'd talk more when I get back next week."

Lexia's eyes lit up. "Really?"

"Yes, really. How much more do you have to do?" He glanced down at his watch.

"Sam's going to close up, so we can leave anytime."

"Good. I'd rather be early than late. Are you ready?"

She took a deep breath. "Yes." Or at least she hoped so.

Chapter 15

Lexia stepped out of the town car on shaky legs and stared up at the hotel. She couldn't believe they were staying at the Ritz-Carlton. Or that they'd made it in one piece. Even at midnight, there was still some traffic and the way the driver had woven in and out of the lanes nearly gave her a heart attack. With this being her first trip to New York, she wanted to see all the sights, but the man had made her so nervous, she'd ended up closing her eyes for a good portion of the ride. Khalil, on the other hand, hadn't even flinched.

"Are you okay, Lexia?"

She leveled a glare at the departing car service driver, looked up at Khalil and shook her head. Her heart still beat double time in her chest and her hands shook.

Khalil chuckled. "Come on. Let's get you settled in, baby."

A bellhop collected their luggage and she followed Khalil to the registration desk. Other than having to ask the clerk to repeat information twice so he could understand, the process went smoothly.

They took the elevator to the twenty-second floor and entered an elegant one-bedroom suite overlooking Central Park that was larger than her condo. After getting up early and traveling all day, Lexia was bone tired, but she was also starving. She dropped her purse and tote on a chair and fell across the bed.

Khalil chuckled. He came and stretched out next to her. He pushed her hair back and lowered his mouth to hers.

Lexia's fatigue melted away and desire flared. She reached up, hooked her hand behind his head and pulled him closer. She ran her other hand over his shoulders and down his muscular arm. He slid his hand beneath her top, caressed her spine, torso and around to her breasts. A knock sounded. She groaned and tapped Khalil on the shoulder.

He lifted his head and frowned. "What?"

She spelled door, sat up and adjusted her clothes.

He sighed, scooted off the bed and went to let the bell-hop in. He gave the man a tip, closed the door and came back to the bed. "Now, where were we?"

She gave him a sultry smile and crooked a finger.

He grinned and kissed her back down onto the bed.

Lexia forgot about being tired, hungry and everything else, except the delicious sensations coursing through her body. In a matter of moments they were both naked and she was riding him in the middle of the king-size bed. His hands gripped her buttocks as he moved with deep, steady strokes. Her head fell back and she held on to his shoulders as each thrust drove her closer and closer to the edge. He reached down and pressed his thumb against her clit, taking her higher with slow, sensual circles.

Their breathing grew ragged, echoing loudly in the otherwise quiet room. Khalil lifted his head and pulled her into a kiss so erotic it made her head spin. He plunged faster and faster until she convulsed all around him, spasms of ecstasy rocketing through her body.

Khalil followed her over the edge, thrusting so deeply that she came again in a rush of pleasure so strong she almost toppled off his body.

Lexia collapsed on top of him as their bodies shuddered intensely and he held her tightly. Neither of them moved for several minutes. She started to get up and he stayed her. She tried to tell him that she didn't want to cause him any pain, but he didn't loosen his grip.

He placed a gentle kiss on her forehead. "I'm fine, Lexia. I just want to hold you, sweetheart."

Her breath caught upon seeing the tender look on his

face and she lost a piece of her heart. Afraid he might read her thoughts, she laid her head on his shoulder and closed her eyes. *This wasn't supposed to happen.* Now what? She certainly couldn't tell him. Her breathing slowed and she drifted off to sleep.

Lexia woke up bleary-eyed and alone in the bed. She shifted to see the clock on the nightstand. Only an hour had passed. She glanced down at the sheet covering her body, puzzled. Had Khalil picked her up and put her under the covers? Shaking her head, she left the bed, dressed and went in search of Khalil. He was standing shirtless in front of the window in the living room with his hands in his pockets, seemingly deep in thought. She slipped her arms around his waist and leaned her cheek against his back.

"Hey, sleepyhead." Khalil shifted, brought her in front of him and wrapped his arms around her.

At length, she turned in his arms and signed that she was hungry.

"We can order room service." He walked over and found the menu, brought it back to where she stood and opened it.

The hotel had quite a few selections that looked good, but with it being so late, she didn't want anything too heavy. She pointed to the chicken noodle soup.

"I'll have the same."

She called in the order and they resumed their position at the window. They stood staring out at the black velvet night and lighted park. And just like when they sat out on his balcony, contentment rose in Lexia so sharply it scared her. She was in too deep.

Khalil jerked upright in bed. He swore he heard something. The same thing had happened two days ago while at the gym. The muffled sound of weights dropping had caught his attention, as did intermittent snatches of voices during his conversation with Cameron yesterday. His heart pounded in his chest and his breathing increased. He glanced over his shoulder at Lexia sleeping soundly. During his doctor's visit, Dr. Moyer had told Khalil that the tear in his left ear was healing nicely and that he might begin to hear some sounds. However, there had been little change in his right ear. He rose silently, crossed the carpeted floor and stood in the middle of the dark room, straining his ears. Nothing.

He went into the bathroom, closed the door softly and braced his hands on the marble sink. What if that's all he'd ever hear—just bits of muffled sounds? The fear that he would never regain his hearing came back full force. He lowered his head and pushed the negative thoughts aside. *The tear is healing. He said it's coming back. You're not going crazy.*

Khalil straightened and turned on the shower. He searched through his toiletry bag for the earplugs that he hated having to wear, inserted them and stepped into the warm spray. While washing up, his mind drifted to Lexia. After eating the soup, they'd had a second round with her bent over the bed as he took her from behind. Totally spent, they had promptly gone to sleep. He hadn't planned for them to have sex fifteen minutes after arriving at the hotel, but when she gave him that sexy smile and kissed him with a passion that sent electricity through his body, he'd lost control. She was the only woman who had ever been able to penetrate his ironclad will and his feelings were getting more complicated by the minute. He told himself that he could keep his body and heart separate—he'd never had a problem before—but each touch, each kiss and each time he entered her body chipped away at the invisible wall he had built and blurred the lines until he could no longer tell the difference.

Khalil shut off the water, grabbed the towel he had placed outside the door and dried off. He brushed his teeth, then padded naked back into the bedroom and dressed in sweats and a long-sleeved tee. Lexia still hadn't stirred. He wrote a note letting her know that he was going for a run and placed it on his pillow, then stuck his phone, wallet and room key into his pocket and quietly left the room.

Not working out for over a month had tested his patience and he couldn't take it any longer. Once at the park, he took a minute to stretch. A brisk breeze kicked up and, though the sun peeked through the clouds, the temperatures were still cool. Khalil finished his warm-up and started a slow jog. Though it was seven thirty on a Saturday morning, several people had the same idea. He forced himself to take it easy and stopped after a mile. His cardio sucked and he hoped it wouldn't take long to build his endurance again.

When Khalil got back, Lexia was sitting up in bed with the sheet covering her. "Good morning, sunshine."

Lexia gave him a look and reached for her phone. "It's Saturday and you said this thing didn't start until seven this evening. Why are you up so early? And are you supposed to be running?"

Khalil grinned. "I only jogged a mile…a *slow* jog." He folded his arms. "I take it you're not a morning person. And I rarely sleep in. I guess it's probably from all the years of modeling. I had to be up early for a lot of the photo shoots or when traveling to back-to-back assignments."

"I get to the café every morning around five, so I take full advantage of my weekends. You should learn to do the same sometimes."

"I'll see what I can do," he said with a chuckle. She stretched and the sheet dropped slightly, giving him a flash of her full breasts before she tightened it. His body reacted with lightning speed.

"So, what are we doing until the event?"

He shrugged. "Whatever you want to do since it's your first time in the city."

She angled her head thoughtfully. "We have to go to Central Park, of course, the Empire State Building and, maybe Times Square. I need to have some time to do my hair, so I want to be back a little early."

She had mirrored pretty much every place he had in mind. "Okay. I need to shower again. But you can go first, if you want. Or…" He wiggled his eyebrows.

"Or you can use one bathroom, while I use the other. I want to see the city, remember?" Lexia asked, shaking her head.

"Can't fault a brother for trying." If they showered together, they'd never make it out of the suite. "We'll go down for breakfast when you're ready. Make sure you wear your walking shoes. You can take this bathroom and I'll use the other one." Khalil gathered his clothes and toiletries, then left her alone to get dressed. The memories of their last shower together remained crystal clear in his mind and it took everything in him not to turn back.

To save time, they ate a light breakfast in the hotel. On his past visits to the city, Khalil typically walked the seventeen blocks to Times Square, but after the run, he didn't want to overdo it and arranged for transportation through the hotel. The driver dropped them off at Junior's Restaurant on Broadway and he smiled at Lexia's excitement.

Lexia turned in a slow circle with wide eyes. "This is fabulous." She took several pictures and had Khalil take one of her with the crowd of people in the background. Because of the noise, they decided that she would use texting for communication. "I can't believe I'm on Broadway."

He took her hand and they strolled up the street. When

they got to the corner, she stopped short. Khalil glanced down to see her staring. "What?"

"Is that where they drop the ball on New Year's Eve?"

"Yes."

"We have to take a picture." She held her phone up and moved it around, apparently trying to get a good angle. She frowned. "You're too tall. All I'm getting is your chest."

He laughed. "I could always pick you up."

She leveled him with a glare that dared him to try it.

"My arms are longer. Let me do it." He took her phone, squatted down and held it up. As he snapped it, instead of looking into the camera, he impulsively kissed her cheek. Being around Lexia brought out a playful side in him that only his family saw. She whipped her head in his direction and, taking full advantage, he placed a kiss on her lips while taking another picture. Lexia touched her fingers to his lips and it sent a jolt straight through his chest. Fighting to keep the intense emotions at bay, he said, "We have a lot of ground to cover and a short amount of time to do it, so we'd better keep moving."

They were able to hit Rockefeller Center, the Empire State Building and take a carriage ride around Central Park to round out their mini sightseeing tour.

When they got back to the hotel, Lexia yawned. "Thank you so much for the tour. I especially loved the carriage ride." She came up on tiptoe and kissed him. "Since it's only a little after three, I think I'm going to lie down for a while. My time clock is all messed up."

Khalil circled his arms around her. "You're welcome. What time do you want me to wake you?"

"Four thirty, if I'm not already up. What are you going to do?"

"I brought some work with me." Though he'd read what she said, he had caught a couple of words. However, he decided not to say anything to anyone until he could hear consistently. Right now, the sounds came in and out—more out—and he didn't want to get excited just yet.

"Okay. I'll see you in a bit."

He bent and kissed her softly. "Sleep well." He watched her until she disappeared into the bedroom, then dropped down into the nearest chair and buried his head in his hands. He was falling in love with her. *How did I let this happen?*

Lexia added the rhinestone pin to her hair and surveyed the style. She had done one large French braid across the front and swept the curly mass up at the top of her head. She left the bathroom and sat on the bench at the foot of the bed to put on the four-inch silver sandals with matching rhinestones across the toe strap. She fastened the buckle at the ankle, stood and walked over to the full-length mirror. She had chosen a sleeveless, long black A-line silhouette evening gown designed with a rhinestone embellished illusion lace front and back, sweetheart bustline and thigh-high slit. She heard Khalil gasp sharply and rotated to face him. He'd paired a white tuxedo jacket with the black pants and the photos she'd seen of him in formal wear didn't come close to capturing his masculine beauty. She held out her arms.

"You look absolutely stunning." His gaze made a slow tour down her body and back up again. "And you're about two seconds from me skipping this event and taking that gown off you."

The blatant desire in his eyes sent heat humming through her body. "We're going to be late."

Khalil gave her a wicked grin. "Probably."

Lexia took a step back and held up her hand. "Do you know how long it took me to get my hair up like this? If you mess it up, I'm going to hurt you."

He closed the distance between them. "I certainly don't want that, so how about this? We go, mingle for a while, then come back and I take it off." His lips and tongue blazed a trail down her throat while his hand slipped inside the slit and caressed her thigh. "Then I'm going to start at your feet and kiss my way up your sexy body. I'll linger here…" He moved his hand to her inner thigh. "And here." His fingers grazed her core.

She sucked in a deep breath. His words had her so turned on that if they stood here one moment longer she was going to rip the dress off herself and save him the trouble. She closed her eyes briefly to gain control.

He straightened and stepped back. "So every time our eyes meet, know that's what I'll be thinking."

Oh Lawd! That's all she needed to hear. To distract herself, she crossed over to the bed to get her purse. "Can I ask you a question?"

"Sure."

"How do you feel about what happened with the woman you were supposed to escort?"

Khalil's jaw tightened. "It was for her benefit, not mine. Besides, if I had escorted her, I wouldn't be here with you. And if I had to choose between you two, I'd choose you every time." He pressed a kiss to her lips.

Just like that Lexia lost another chunk of her heart.

Chapter 16

"Ready?" Khalil asked.

Not trusting herself to speak, she nodded. Khalil was quiet as they walked down the carpeted corridor and in the elevator as they rode to the bottom. Although he hadn't said it, she sensed his nervousness. But then, she'd be the same way if she had to enter a ballroom full of people and couldn't hear anything, especially since most, if not all, of the attendees would know her. At best, it would be overwhelming and, at worst, terrifying. She just prayed no one would be outright rude. They exited the elevator in the lobby and Khalil headed for the front doors. She tapped him on the shoulder.

Before she asked, Khalil said, "It was originally scheduled to be here, but far more people RSVP'd than originally anticipated and the Ritz doesn't have a large enough ballroom. So it's at the Marriott right down the street." He glanced down and stopped walking. "Are you going to be okay walking in those shoes? If not, I'll arrange for transportation."

Lexia waved him off and shook her head. "I'll be fine. But coming back might be another story."

He chuckled. "Then, I'll make sure we get a ride." He slung his arm around her shoulder. "I could always carry you."

She shook her head quickly again. Seeing the amusement on his face, she pointed. "Walk." She could imagine what would happen if he carried her down the street. People would stop, whip out their smartphones and start snapping pictures. Before she and Khalil made it back to the hotel, the photos would be uploaded to every social media outlet known to man.

Khalil shrugged. "Just sayin'."

As promised, after a short walk they entered the second hotel and followed the directions to the Grand Salon. Lexia and Khalil hadn't taken more than two steps into the exquisitely decorated ballroom when all eyes turned their way and every conversation within a twenty-foot radius halted. There had to be at least three or four hundred people mingling. She felt Khalil stiffen and gave his hand a reassuring squeeze. Moments later, a light brown–skinned woman with a weave clear down to her waist, wearing a fire-engine-red halter dress that dipped to her waist and clung to her tall, slender frame rushed over and nearly knocked Lexia over as she draped herself all over Khalil.

"Oh, Khalil, honey, I'm so glad to see you. I heard about the accident and I've been so worried about you. You haven't returned any of my calls."

Lexia lifted a brow.

Khalil gently removed the woman's arms. "Hello, Tasha." He took a step closer to Lexia and reached for her hand. "Lexia, this is Tasha Ayers. She's one of the models working with the teen program. Tasha, this is Lexia Daniels."

"It's nice to meet you, Tasha," Lexia said. "This sounds like an awesome program and the room looks fabulous."

Tasha glanced down at their entwined hands, then up at Khalil and Lexia. "Same here."

However, her voice was about as cold as New York in December, leaving Lexia to wonder if Tasha and Khalil had dated in the past. Tasha started talking again, gesturing around the room, her face turned away from Khalil. Lexia heard him sigh. "Excuse me, Tasha."

"Yes," she said impatiently.

Lexia mentally counted to ten. She'd only been in the room a minute—much too early to give someone a set down. She eased the phone out of Khalil's hand and held it up. "You said you heard about his accident, then you know that his hearing was affected by the blast. Please use this cell to communicate with him. Just talk and he'll be able to read it on his phone."

"Oh, I thought all that was taken care of and that you were fine now."

"What is it that you need, Tasha?" Khalil asked.

"I was going to…" She waved a dismissive hand. "Never mind, I'll ask someone else." She shoved the phone back into Lexia's hand and strutted off.

"So, I guess this is how it's going to be. My hearing was damaged, not my damn brain," he muttered.

Lexia surveyed the people standing nearby. All wore wary expressions, as if they couldn't decide whether or not to approach, and she could feel the tension rolling off him in waves. She sighed inwardly. Attempting to make him feel better, she said with a roll of her eyes, "Tasha seems a little high maintenance. Trust me, you'd probably be better off letting her find someone else to do her bidding." That earned her a small smile.

He brought her hand to his lips. "Come on, baby. Let me introduce you to the kids." A man appeared and offered them flutes of champagne. Khalil handed one to Lexia and took one for himself.

He led her over to a group of four teens—two girls and two boys—who looked to be between the ages of fifteen and seventeen. Unlike the previous gawkers, their faces lit up and they rushed to meet Khalil and Lexia with wide smiles. Lexia could definitely see why an agency wanted to put them in front of a camera. They were gorgeous children and all of them towered over Lexia. One girl held up a notepad. Obviously, she'd been waiting for Khalil.

Mr. Gray, we were so sad to hear about your accident, but we're glad you're doing better and are here tonight.

They took turns writing on the pad until Khalil told them about the app. Unlike the adults, the teens whipped out their phones and downloaded the app.

After Khalil introduced Lexia, the other girl asked, "Is she your girlfriend?"

Khalil's glance slid to Lexia's briefly. "Yeah, she is. Now get out of my business," he said teasingly. He asked them how they were doing in school, about their various modeling assignments and generally how they were doing overall.

Lexia sipped her champagne while thinking about Khalil's pronouncement that she was his girlfriend. She didn't know what she expected him to say—they hadn't really defined their relationship—but did he really think of her in those terms or had he said it for the kids' benefit?

Although she'd never said it aloud, deep down she longed for the kind of loving relationship she'd seen with her parents and grandparents, as well as children. Being an only child had been lonesome sometimes, and she always dreamed she would have at least two. But after her divorce, she had put those fantasies aside. Spending these last few weeks with Khalil, traveling first-class and staying in a five-star hotel, and now hearing him publicly declare her as *his* did something to her insides. When she agreed to keep seeing him, he'd mentioned wanting her, but that didn't mean he would be looking for something long-term or permanent.

Khalil introduced her to a few more people, some pleasant and others not so much.

He left her for a moment to speak with an older man, but his heated gaze slid her way more than once. *I'm going to start at your feet and kiss my way up your sexy body.* His words rushed back to her.

"It's really a shame about what happened to him."

Lexia turned slowly. Tasha. "What do you mean?"

Tasha gestured. "I mean…look at him. He'll never be able to fit in anymore and he was one of the best. It's such a waste."

She chuckled bitterly. "You're talking about him as if he's dead. Nothing has changed, he just has some hearing loss." Lexia wanted to shake some sense into this woman.

Tasha looked Lexia up and down with disdain. "So, are you like his interpreter or something?"

Lexia angled her head and wondered how much trouble she would be in if she ruined the fund-raiser by smacking this woman. "Or something."

Tasha glanced Khalil's way again as he started toward them. "Better you than me. Well, take good care of him for me."

She pasted a smile on her face and said in a saccharine-sweet voice, "Oh, I plan to take very good care of him… *for me.*" She gave Tasha a pointed glare to make sure the woman got her meaning, then strode off.

Khalil met her halfway. "What was that all about?"

"Nothing."

He studied her, as if trying to determine the truth and, seemingly satisfied, nodded.

She hooked her arm in his and they continued to stroll across the ballroom. They passed a popular male model with a beautiful young woman on his arm. "That's Rayford Arrington, right? Wasn't he up on drunk driving charges last year and some kind of disturbance in a club a few months ago?"

"Yes."

"Do you know the woman with him?" His features hardened and he didn't answer for a moment.

Finally, he said, "Yes. That's Rosalyn Stills. She's the woman I was supposed to escort."

Lexia's shocked gaze flew to Khalil's. "And her agent decided that being seen with him would be good for her career?" She shook her head. Obviously, she had a lot to learn about this business.

"It may do something to her career. I just hope this doesn't end it before it starts, because she's a nice person. But she's not my concern." Khalil smiled down at Lexia. "I think it's time for dinner." He escorted her to a table in the front of the room to be seated for dinner.

During the meal of chicken breast stuffed with spinach and cheese, roasted red potatoes and steamed vegetables, conversation flowed around the table, but only one person went out of his way to include Khalil. Lexia couldn't believe their rudeness.

Afterward, there were speeches by former and current models, agents, a parent and a teen. Each of them praised the program, but it was the parent that left Lexia with her mouth hanging open as she introduced Khalil as the founder of the program.

Lexia playfully hit Khalil on the thigh under the table. "You didn't tell me you started the program."

Khalil shrugged.

"I think you're supposed to get up there and talk."

He pushed back from the table and made his way to the stage amid a standing ovation. "Thank you." He waited until the audience sat. "I appreciate all of you more than I can say. I may have started the program, but it's the staff, parents and students who make this work." He thanked the many supporters, cited statistics and success stories, and stressed the need for ongoing funding.

When he finished, Lexia was on her feet with everyone else in the room. He returned to his seat and shortly after, the dancing started. She hadn't been dancing in a while and really wanted to hit the floor, but didn't want Khalil to feel uncomfortable. A jazzy ballad came on and she thought it would be the perfect song. "Dance with me."

Khalil stared at her a lengthy minute and several expressions crossed his face—anxiety, uncertainty and for a split second, the same fear she remembered seeing right after the accident. Finally, he stood and extended his hand. "You're going to have to take the lead on this one."

She smiled. "No problem. You'll get the next one."

He returned her smile, led her out to the floor and pulled her into his arms.

Lexia started a slow sway that he could easily keep up with and rested her head against his shoulder. She loved the feel of his strong arms around her and they continued to dance as the DJ played two more slow tunes. In the middle of the third tune, she detected a shift in the way he held her. He gathered her closer and his hands moved slowly up and down her back. She lifted her head and their gazes locked. He silently communicated a reminder of what he'd said before they left and her body responded in kind.

He bent close to her ear. "It's time for me to take off this dress."

She lifted her head and their lips were a breath apart. Heat shot through her.

"Yes? No?"

"Yes." *And the sooner the better.*

Khalil did his best not to rip the dress from Lexia's body as soon as the hotel room door closed, which was why he hadn't moved. His body had been at a slow burn from the moment he'd seen her in the sexy outfit. Every step had given him a flash of her sleek, brown legs and it had taken everything within him not to drag her up to the nearest room and show her just how much he desired her.

He crossed the room to where she stood, mesmerized by all that she was. She'd stayed by his side, subtly kept him aware of his surroundings—though sounds continued to filter in and out—and been warm and charming, even to the few people who hadn't deserved it. He still didn't believe her claims that nothing had happened between her and Tasha. He'd known Tasha for a good fifteen years and had always kept his distance because drama was her middle name.

But Lexia was another story. He couldn't stay away from her even if he'd tried. And he had. She smiled up at him, placed her hands on his chest and moved them up and around his neck. A sensation he had never experienced gripped him. Khalil pushed it aside, preferring not to deal with the emotional turmoil her touch elicited inside him. The only thing he wanted to focus on right now was slowly stripping away the soft material and pleasuring her until neither of them could move. He hardened immediately.

Khalil kissed her deeply, then turned her around. He undid the hook and eased the zipper down the lace bodice that stopped just above her shapely bottom, pausing to feather kisses down her spine. The knowledge that she didn't have on a bra aroused him further. He ran his fingers lightly up and down her back and felt her tremble. He pulled the open halves down her arms and it pooled at her waist. Lowering his head, he trailed kisses over her shoulders and neck, and reached around to knead and massage her breasts.

Lexia's head fell back against his chest and she cried out.

He froze. His heart started pounding. *I heard her!* A different set of emotions engulfed him. Continuing his quest,

Khalil kissed down the length of her arms, removed the dress and draped it over the back of the sofa, leaving her wearing only a pair of skimpy black panties and her silver shoes. He shrugged off his jacket and tie and tossed them on top of the dress. Rotating her to face him, he scanned her scantily clad body. "You are absolute perfection, sweet baby."

"So are you," Lexia spelled. She undid the buttons on his shirt, pushed it off his shoulders and kissed her way across his chest and down the center of his body to his belt buckle.

Khalil sucked in a sharp breath. He swept her up into his arms, crossed the suite to the bedroom and laid her in the center of the bed. He kicked off his shoes, positioned himself at the foot of the bed and admired the alluring picture she made. He climbed onto the bed, lifted her foot and kissed her ankle. He repeated the same gesture on the other foot, and then, holding her legs apart, alternately kissed his way up both inner legs to her center. He flicked his tongue against the spot and her hips flew off the bed.

Leaving her a moment, he shed his pants, socks and briefs, and donned a condom. He came back to the bed. "Now, where was I?" He lowered his body over hers, being careful not to put all his weight on her and slanted his mouth over hers, their tongues tangling and teasing. She captured his tongue and gently sucked, and he groaned. Sliding down her body, he pulled her panties down and off.

Lexia held up her small foot with her perfectly painted purple nails and the rhinestones shimmered in the light. "My shoes."

Khalil shook his head. "Leave them on." He traced a path with his tongue from her ankle to the back of her knee, placed a lingering kiss, resumed his course and ended at her core, where she was already wet. Her aroused scent filled his nostrils. He had to taste her. He hooked her legs over

his shoulders and settled between her thighs. At the first
stroke of his tongue, she stiffened and he heard it again—
she screamed. He swirled deeper and moved with long, bold
strokes from bottom to top and back again.

He slipped two fingers inside her opening as he took
the tiny bud between his lips. She was so sweet, so respon-
sive. He quickened the pace and her thighs tightened on his
shoulders, her hips arched off the bed and her body shook
uncontrollably as she climaxed all around him. He slowed
his movements, withdrew and slid up her body.

Lexia's eyes fluttered open and connected with his. A
soft smile touched her lips and she leaned up and kissed
him.

That funny feeling in his chest came back and Khalil
forced it down, trying to convince himself that this was
nothing more than a strong physical attraction. Holding
her gaze, he shifted his lower body and entered her with
one long thrust, snugly fit in the place he couldn't seem to
get enough of. He retreated almost to the tip, then thrust
himself completely inside her again. She caught his rhythm
and he guided her hips as she lifted to meet each stroke. He
watched her rapturous expression and his release struggled
to rise to the surface.

"Don't stop, baby," she chanted.

With each stroke, Khalil felt her pulling everything out
of him. And when his release came, it was intense and all-
encompassing. For the first time in almost six weeks, he
heard his own voice as he yelled out her name. Another
set of emotions took hold and joy filled his soul. She came
right with him, deep tremors taking over their bodies. He
couldn't explain this connection or the sensations humming through him. He buried his face in her neck, whis-
pering, murmuring—what, he didn't quite know. Once his
breathing slowed, he withdrew and removed her shoes. He

rolled to his side, taking her with him. They didn't talk—just simply fell asleep in each other's arms.

Khalil didn't know how much time had passed when he felt Lexia's warm lips against his cheek. He didn't move or open his eyes.

"I love you."

His heart stopped and started up again, and he forced himself to stay still. She loved him? Love came with too many complications and he didn't do *love*. But he didn't want to hurt her, nor could he stay away. Now what the hell was he supposed to do?

Chapter 17

For the next three days after returning from New York, Khalil threw himself back into work, finalizing details on new equipment and interviewing for a new manager. He'd also gone to the police station to identify and retrieve his property and was working with them to get his money back. He had hoped by staying busy, he wouldn't have to think about his dilemma with Lexia. He hadn't talked to her since dropping her off on Sunday evening and missed her more than he thought possible. Every time he closed his eyes, he saw her beautiful face, smelled her intoxicating citrusy fragrance, felt her heated touch and remembered each erotic moment of the weekend. Even now, arousal flowed through his veins.

His cell buzzed. Although his hearing had returned pretty well in his left ear, he hadn't told anyone and the staff continued to utilize technology for communication. He read the text from the receptionist, letting him know that Cameron was on his way up. After much consideration, Cameron fit far better than the other candidates and, despite his lack of knowledge of fitness, Khalil suspected it wouldn't take long for the man to get up to speed. According to Cameron's former employer, Cameron had had a stellar record prior to the tragedy.

Khalil stood and rounded the desk when Cameron knocked on the partially open door. "Come on in." They shook and Khalil gestured him to a chair. "Thanks for coming."

Cameron lowered his large body into the chair. "Thanks for the invitation."

He went back to his desk. "I'd like to offer you the new manager's position. I understand that the salary is a little lower than your previous job, but I'm hoping you'll take the position."

Cameron leaned back in his chair and didn't immediately comment. Then, "I don't mean to look a gift horse in the mouth, but are you doing this to try to win some points with Lexia? No offense."

"None taken." Khalil had to hand it to the man. He didn't pull any punches, especially where Lexia was concerned. Cameron had made that clear on their first meeting. But this was business and Khalil never let anything influence him when it came to his livelihood. "This has nothing to do with Lexia. Only your résumé."

They engaged in a staredown for several seconds before he nodded. "Then I'll take the job. I really appreciate you taking a chance on me."

"Like I said, you have an impressive résumé. The gym doesn't open for another month, but I would like for you to start immediately. You can train here and be ready to hit the ground running in June."

Cameron shook his head. "I can start right now, if you want," he said with a chuckle.

Khalil grinned, stood and extended his hand. "Welcome to Maximum Burn. We'll take a tour, come back up here so I can show you the design of the new facility, then I'll introduce you to Felicia and she'll give you some paperwork to fill out. I'd also like to know if you'd be available to meet later this week about the project you mentioned for the homeless. I'm going to see if my brothers and sisters will help."

Cameron stood, seemingly in shock. "Are you serious? Wow." He pumped Khalil's hand so hard Khalil thought it was going to fall off. "Thank you, thank you. Just let me know when."

It took another half hour to complete everything and

Khalil went back to his office. He took his cell out and sent a group text to his siblings. Malcolm was leaving in three weeks for vacation and he wanted to get the ball rolling before then. By the end of the day, he'd heard from everyone and they agreed to meet on Friday evening. Everything seemed to be on track—the progress on the new gym, a new manager, his hearing—except what to do about Lexia. He was honest enough to admit that he had feelings for her, but after his last experience, he had vowed to never again let someone close to his heart. And he'd done fine up to this point. But he couldn't leave things the way they were. It wasn't fair to Lexia. He just needed to come up with a way to tell her he couldn't see her anymore. A churning started in his gut. That prospect didn't sit well, either.

Khalil poked his head in the office that the staff trainers used to let them know he was leaving. Instead of having a manager on duty in the evenings, one or more of the trainers handled that shift on rotation. Khalil usually came in some evenings, as well. He drove home and immediately stepped out onto the terrace off his living room. With the calendar changing to May, the lengthening days made it possible for him to catch the sunset if he got home by seven. He inhaled deeply, grateful for the gift of being able to hear the sound of the ocean crashing against the shore again. He still had concern about what would happen with his right ear, but it was tempered by this small blessing.

His cell buzzed in his pocket and he fished it out. He smiled and shook his head upon seeing his mother's name on the display. She had texted him every couple of days since she and his father left for their ten-day Caribbean cruise. They were due back on Friday and he knew what she wanted. Khalil swiped the screen and tapped on her message.

Hello, son. Your father and I are having a blast. I should be rested enough to visit you on Saturday, so I hope you'll be available. Love you!

She hoped he'd be available? He laughed. That meant he needed to be available on Saturday, no matter what he had planned. He let her know that he'd drive over on Saturday afternoon. He started to tell her about his hearing, but decided to wait and surprise them.

The phone buzzed again and he went still.

Lexia's message dropped down: Hey, baby. Just checking to see if everything is okay.

She had only called him "baby" once during that lovemaking session on Saturday night. The night she had uttered those three words. His thumb hovered over the screen for a few seconds before he replied: I'm good, just catching up on work. He hesitated once more before asking if he could stop by tomorrow after work.

Lexia responded simply, Yes.

That gave him twenty-four hours to come up with a way to let go of the woman who had captured his heart.

Lexia sat in her bedroom Thursday afternoon staring at the photos from New York on her phone. Her weekend with Khalil had been something straight out of a fantasy, from the lavish accommodations and mini city tour to dancing in the middle of an exquisitely decorated ballroom and passionate lovemaking. She would never *ever* forget the night with the shoes. She had been so caught up in the sensations that she had foolishly told him she loved him. Her only saving grace was that he couldn't hear her. It also helped that he had been asleep. She shook her head. *What was I thinking?* She wasn't. Not after the way he'd looked at her afterward and the tender kiss he had given her that had melted her heart. She'd let her emotions spill over and hadn't been able to put them back in the bottle since.

Lexia continued going through the photos and slowed at the ones taken in Times Square, the first one with him playfully kissing her cheek and the one when he'd turned her face to his and kissed her while taking the picture. Of all the moments they had shared, this one was near the top of the list. Over the past several weeks, she had come to realize there was much more to Khalil beneath the sculpted body and handsome face. How on earth was she supposed to resist him? The doorbell rang. She exited out of the photo gallery. When she opened the door and saw Khalil her heart rate increased. It had only been four days since she had seen him, but the excitement bubbling up inside her made it seem longer.

"Hey. Come on in." She stepped back so he could enter.

Khalil brushed a kiss over her lips and crossed the threshold. "Hey."

He took a seat on the sofa and she sat next to him. "Can I get you something?" she spelled.

A faint smile touched his lips. "No, thanks." He grasped her hand. "We need to talk."

"Okay." Lexia reached for her phone and he covered her hand with his.

"We don't need it."

She observed him a moment, and then it dawned on her. "You can hear me?"

He pointed to his left ear. "Just out of this one."

Dread uncoiled in her belly. "How long?"

"It's been in and out for the past several days, but more consistent over the last two."

Had he heard her that night? She was too afraid to ask, not sure she wanted to know the answer. Instead she smiled and kissed him. "I'm really happy for you."

"Thank you."

They lapsed into silence and Lexia sensed something not quite right. "Is there something wrong? You said we needed to talk."

Khalil stared at her a long moment. "We do. I'm not sure where to begin. Lexia, I really enjoy being with you and the time we spent together, but…"

She pulled her hand away. "But what?"

"I don't think…maybe we should…"

Lexia leaned away, then stood. She knew what was coming next. "Maybe we should have some space? Is that what you were going to say?" He didn't comment, but his expression told all. She scrubbed a hand across her forehead and paced. "I don't believe this," she muttered. She whirled on him and pointed a finger his way. "I asked for some space, but *you* came after me. Now all of a sudden you need space. If all you wanted to do was sleep with me then you could have skipped all the pretense."

He jumped up. "It's not like that," he gritted out.

She folded her arms and glared at him. "No? Then please, by all means enlighten me. How is it, *exactly*?"

Khalil held up his palms. "Look, Lexia. I'm sorry. I'm not—"

She chuckled bitterly. "You've got that right."

"I didn't plan for any of this. It wasn't supposed to happen this way," he added softly.

Lexia let out an exasperated sigh. "What way did you think it would turn out? The hand-holding, kissing, spending time together—what was I supposed to think? I actually believed you cared about me, but I guess I was wrong."

He ran a hand down his face. "I do care about you, Lexia, but I can't give you what you want. This isn't like some fairy tale where I can wave a magic wand and make everything perfect."

"I never asked you for a fairy tale." The only thing she had ever asked was that the love she had given be returned to her. She bit back the tears threatening to fall. She refused to let him see her cry. "Was there anything else?"

Khalil closed the distance between them. "Lexia."

"Just go, okay?"

He lifted his hand to touch her face and she moved out of his reach. He dropped his hand to his side, turned on his heel and walked out.

As soon as the door closed softly behind him, the tears she had held at bay came full force. When was she going to learn? Love wasn't meant for her.

Chapter 18

"Khalil!"

Khalil turned at the sound of Brandon's voice. All of his siblings and their spouses were staring at him. "What?"

"I called your name like four times. What is going on? Do we need to use our phones again?" Brandon pulled his out.

"No. I can hear you just fine. And so can my neighbors," he added sarcastically. They had all been surprised when he told them about being able to hear again. But the one thing he wanted to hear was his niece's laughter. She was asleep when Justin and Siobhan arrived and just woke up. He pushed back from the table and plucked her out of Siobhan's arms. "Hey, Miss Nyla. How's my baby girl?" He kissed her soft, brown cheek. She stared up at him with sleepy eyes, then as she recognized him, a wide, toothless smile spread across her face. Nyla reached up and rubbed her hand across his beard. Before he could blink, her chubby hand grabbed his ear and latched on to the diamond stud. "Whoa."

Siobhan carefully removed her hand. "You have to watch her. She's quick."

"I guess so." Khalil held her up and nuzzled her belly. Her sparkling laughter warmed his heart.

"You could have your own little girl," Brandon teased. "Lexia would make a perfect mother."

A sharp pain replaced the warmth. "I didn't ask you all here to get into my personal life."

"No, but you haven't said anything past wanting to get some mobile services in the areas where the homeless congregate," Morgan said. "You've just been staring into space all starry-eyed." She leaned forward. "That means either you're ready to take the plunge, or you messed it up."

Khalil cut Morgan a look.

"Yep, he messed it up." She grinned and rubbed her hands together. "Let's hurry up and get this discussion over with, so we can cut to the juicy stuff."

"Omar, get your wife. As I was saying, I've done some research and found a couple of pretty cool things. One is a mobile shower and the other is a mobile grocery store. Both utilize renovated buses and we could have someone to drive through those areas maybe three times a week. Cameron gave me three neighborhood addresses." He shifted Nyla in his arms, opened a folder and picked up a piece of paper. "I—" Nyla closed her fist around the edge with lightning-speed reflexes. "Look here, little miss," Khalil said with a chuckle. "Can you please let Uncle Khalil finish, then we can play?" She giggled. He shook his head and moved the paper out of her reach. "I took the liberty of checking out the property in those areas and found several abandoned warehouses and a couple of closed-down hotels."

"So, if we buy a couple of them and turn them into transitional living facilities, that would give shelter to at least some," Malcolm said.

"Exactly."

"That's a fabulous idea."

"You read my mind, Faith." He handed Nyla back to Siobhan and picked up his pen.

Omar asked, "How much do you need?"

Khalil smiled. He knew he could count on his family. They went over figures and costs and potential investors and staff for all three projects. Two hours later, he felt they had made good headway and each of the siblings had a task.

"Is there anything else we need to discuss?"

He glanced down at his notes. "I think that's it for now. I

want to run all this by Cameron. He mentioned a family of young people who are on the streets because they lost their parents. The oldest works a few hours a week at a junior college where he takes classes, but the bulk of the money offsets his financial aid. I'd like to see about getting them off the streets and into a home."

Siobhan tapped her hand on the table. "You know, maybe they can work with one of these projects."

"That's a perfect idea." Faith turned toward Brandon. "Or we can get them into the intern program at Grays or with my website design business, depending on their interests and skills."

"I appreciate everybody's willingness to take on this project. We'll meet again in a couple of weeks."

"Now that that's out of the way, Khalil, what did you do to Lexia? Mom said she's an angel." Morgan fixed her gaze on him.

Khalil rolled his eyes. He could imagine everything his mother said after that visit. "Nothing happened. It just didn't work out." *And I can't give her the love she wants… the love she deserves.* At the time, he believed he had done the right thing. The part of him that had been broken when Michaela betrayed him agreed wholeheartedly. But the part of him that craved the touch of sweetness Lexia had brought into his life wasn't so sure.

"You okay, Lexi?"

She rotated her chair. "Hey, Cam. Yeah, I'm fine. Ready to start the week with your new job? Seems like it's going well." She had been surprised but pleased to find out that Khalil had offered Cam the job. Cam had spent the remainder of last week getting acclimated and would start officially today.

"Yeah. So far, so good. I've got a lot to learn about the

fitness parts of the business, but I found a couple of books that should help. Did Khalil tell you that he's going to help with the homeless project we talked about?"

Lexia leaned forward. "No, but that's fantastic." Cameron frowned and she asked, "What?"

"I'm just surprised he didn't tell you since you two seem to be pretty tight."

She shrugged. "I'm sure he'll get around to it." Khalil hadn't mentioned it before his grand announcement four days ago. She tried to keep her tone light because she didn't want Cam to know what had happened. So far, Lexia had been able to keep it together during the day while working, but the weekend had been hard. Cam's voice drew her back into the conversation.

"The other thing I wanted to tell you is I found a place. I won't be able to move in for another two weeks, though."

Lexia smiled, came around the desk and hugged him. "That's great, Cam. I'm so happy everything is going well for you."

He bowed his head. "Thanks. I just want to make Jan proud." He cleared his throat. "The only thing is I didn't keep up with the storage payments and I'll have to start from scratch. It'll be a while before I can get furniture."

Lexia retrieved her purse from a locked drawer, took out a key and handed it to him. "No you won't. I took over the payments last year and everything is there."

"You are a true friend, Lexia," Cam said emotionally.

He clutched the key in his hand as if it was his lifeline, and she supposed it was. Everything in storage connected Cam to the life he used to have. Lexia hoped his future turned out better than hers.

"I'm heading over to the gym now. Is there anything you want me to take care of here when I get back?"

"No, but thanks. I'll make sure to have Mr. Willis leave you a plate."

"I appreciate that. I don't know how I'm ever going to pay you back." Cameron engulfed Lexia in another crushing hug and departed.

She dropped down in her chair and thought about all that had happened since Janice died. Cam had confessed on several occasions that the pain had gotten to be so much that he needed to get lost for a while. Lexia wouldn't mind getting lost for a few days, herself. "It won't be now," she mumbled. The morning rush would begin shortly, and since Jayla didn't come in until ten she had to help Sam.

Out front, Lexia spoke to those occupying tables as she passed. Many of them were regulars, but there were a few unfamiliar faces. She jumped right in, taking orders, filling coffee mugs and carrying plates.

She dropped off an order and met Sam two tables over. "Sam, if you'll take the order at table six, I'll clean off this one."

"Got it." Sam left the stacked dishes and hurried off.

Lexia placed the dishes in a large dishpan, turned, and her gaze collided with Khalil's. *What is he doing here?* Striving to maintain a professional edge, she pointed to a table. "Have a seat and someone will be with you in a moment." As she passed him, she felt the heat of his stare on her back. In the kitchen, she placed the dishpan in the sink and braced her hands on the edge. Just the sight of him in the jeans and silk pullover tee still sent her body into overdrive, and as much as she wanted to hate him, she couldn't turn her feelings off. She stayed in the kitchen a moment longer and hoped that Sam had already taken his order.

She should have known better. Sam pretended to be busy on the other side of the café and wouldn't even make eye contact with Lexia. Sighing inwardly, Lexia walked over to the table.

"What can I get you?"

"The coffee cake, tea and five minutes of your time."

"I'll bring your order in a moment."

Khalil grasped her hand. "And your time?"

"No," she whispered, and pulled away.

"Lexia, baby…" Regret flickered in his eyes.

"Please don't." She blinked back the tears, spun on her heel and fled to the back. She let the wall take her weight and buried her head in her hands.

"Are you okay, Lexi?" Sam draped a comforting arm around Lexia's shoulder.

She nodded quickly and wiped her eyes with the backs of her hands. "I will be. I think I just need to get away for a few days."

"You're more than welcome to use our place in Santa Barbara. I know my parents won't be using it anytime soon. And my brother's kids are still in school, so the place is empty."

The prospect of spending a few days in the beachfront property to get her mind together sounded like an excellent idea. "Normally, I'd say no, but this time, I think I'll take you up on your offer. Do you think you can handle things around here for the rest of the week?"

"Of course, hon. I'll see if Jayla can work a few extra hours in the morning, and Mr. Willis's grandson will be here in the afternoon."

She smiled weakly. "Thanks, Sam."

"You know I'm here for you. I'll call to make sure everything is ready for you. You want to leave tonight or tomorrow?"

"I'll wait until tomorrow."

"Okay."

"Um…can you take Khalil his order, please? I just can't do this right now."

"Sure." Sam started off, stopped and turned around. "For what it's worth, I still believe the two of you belong together. He wanted me to make sure you were all right and he looks about as miserable as you."

Lexia didn't comment. She didn't think she would ever feel as much pain as she had after what her ex put her through. But she was wrong. Dead wrong.

She stayed in her office for the remainder of the day and made sure to leave before Cameron came back. He'd find out soon enough, but she didn't want him to jeopardize his new job.

Tuesday midday, Lexia parked in the driveway of the beautiful home and opened the envelope Sam had given her. Inside she found a set of keys and some information on nearby places. Leave it to Sam to provide the equivalent of a travel package. Smiling, she took out the keys, grabbed her bags and let herself in. As soon as she stepped inside, the tension she'd been carrying around started to ease.

"Wow." The glass doors and windows in the living room provided a stunning ocean view and the area had a built-in fireplace. She set her bags down and continued with her self-guided tour. The large kitchen was equipped with modern appliances, had a center counter with bar stools and a banquet table for dining while looking out at the water and opened to a cozy family room. She retraced her steps, took the stairs to midlevel and found three bedrooms and a hall bathroom. The master suite sat on the upper level, complete with a king-size bed, wet bar, coffeemaker and refrigerator. It had a sitting area with more comfortable seating and a corner work desk. The en suite bathroom was no less elegant with its walk-in shower and large tub placed beneath a picture window.

Lexia pulled out her phone and sent a text to Sam to let her know that she had arrived safely and to thank her again for the offer. She loped back down the stairs, unloaded the groceries she'd purchased on the way, then grabbed the envelope and went outside to the back deck, which sat directly on the beach.

She leafed through the information on places to visit and eat, set them aside and unfolded Sam's note. Her smile faded. The bold handwriting on the paper belonged to Khalil, not Sam. Apparently, her friend hadn't given up on her matchmaking campaign. She started to ball it up and toss it in the garbage can, but stopped in midcrumple and straightened the sheet.

Lexia,
I know I hurt you. Believe me, that was never my intention. Contrary to what you believe, I do care about you…very much and I'd like a chance to explain. Khalil

Lexia leaned her head back against the cushion and closed her eyes. *I do care about you, Lexia, but I can't give you what you want. This isn't like some fairy tale where I can wave a magic wand and make everything perfect.* His cutting words played in her mind. What else was there to explain?

She toed off her shoes and socks, stepped off the deck and sauntered close to the water's edge. The sun shone overhead, but the noon temperatures hovered at just about seventy degrees with a slight breeze. She stood there watching the soft waves crash over the shore and trying to block out everything except the beauty around her. Lexia lowered herself to the sand and let handfuls of the grains seep slowly through her fists. Soon she lost track of time, the sounds around her disappeared and only her inner thoughts remained. Laughter snatched her back into the present.

Lexia glanced up in time to see a couple jogging past. She stood, dusted off her hands and went back into the house. She hadn't eaten and her stomach was sending a loud reminder. She settled on a light meal of chicken soup and half a turkey sandwich. Afterward, she powered up her laptop to check her emails and work on the cookbook she had started. She'd given Jayla a few simple recipes that the young woman and her friends had raved over. Since then, Jayla had been bugging her to write a book for college students and teasingly referred to it as *Cooking for the Domestically Challenged College Student*. So Lexia decided to give it a try. However, today she couldn't concentrate and gave up after an hour. She tried listening to music and reading to occupy her mind, but nothing helped. She went up to the master suite and sat out on the balcony, but all it did was remind her of cuddling with Khalil and him kissing her. Why couldn't she stop thinking about him? Lexia figured by leaving LA for a while, she would be able to escape the pain that plagued her day and night. However, the memories had traveled the distance right alongside her. She hadn't counted on not being able to outrun her feelings.

Khalil sat at his parents' kitchen table Wednesday morning pushing around the food on his plate. His mother had asked him to stop by before going to work and in his present mood, he should have figured a way to decline. Nearly a week had passed and he hadn't made any headway in fixing the mess he'd created in his life.

"You're not eating." His mother slid into the chair next to him.

"I'm not that hungry." He put the fork down.

She clasped her hands around the mug of coffee in front of her and observed him. "Are you still in pain or are you worried about what's going to happen with your other ear?"

"I'm not in pain and I'm just going to wait and see what happens." True, he did have some concerns about the prospect of surgery, but not having Lexia in his life weighed heaviest on his mind at the moment. "You asked me to stop by. Is something going on?"

"That's what I'd like to know."

Oh brother.

"I'm worried about you, Khalil."

He let out a short bark of laughter. "You just saw me on Saturday. I'm fine."

"And you'd be happy if you straightened out things between you and Lexia." She picked up her coffee and took a sip.

"What are you talking about? I'm happy," he lied. Khalil hadn't mentioned anything to his parents about the breakup. He only told his siblings because he knew they'd camp out at his house until he did, especially Siobhan and Brandon. The two of them took being the oldest to a whole new level.

She drilled him with a look. "Khalil Marcellus Gray, I saw those pictures of you and Lexia in New York. You were happy *then*."

He winced. He hated when she called him by his full name. She was right. He had been happier than he could remember.

She covered his hand with hers. "Who was she, sweetheart?"

Khalil's brows knit together. "Who was she, who?"

"The woman who broke your heart."

He froze. He had never told anyone what happened in

Mexico, not even Brandon, as close as they were. "What makes you think someone broke my heart?"

"When you came home from Mexico after your last modeling assignment there, I noticed you weren't as playful, and the light that had always been in your eyes had dimmed. Oh, you did a good job covering it up, but I saw it. I wanted to ask you about it, but your father said you'd share it when you were ready."

She had described him to a tee and he still wasn't ready.

"I know you're in love with Lexia, can see it as clear as glass," she added with a chuckle. Then she sobered, reached over and placed a motherly palm against his cheek. "Don't let fear steal another moment of your life, sweetheart. Yes, there is always a risk when it comes to love, but the payoff is always worth it." She patted his hand. "Now, finish up your food. I have a feeling you're going to need all your strength to get Lexia back."

Khalil shook his head and chuckled. "I love you, Mom." What else could he say?

"I love you more."

After finishing breakfast and kissing his mother goodbye, he sat parked in his car outside the house trying to determine his next move. As much as he hated to admit it, his mother had been right. He was afraid. Afraid that if he let a woman get too close, he would suffer the same heartbreak as before. Now he faced a greater fear—losing Lexia. He drummed his fingers on the steering wheel. Cameron had told Khalil that Lexia was gone on vacation, but he didn't know where. However, Sam would know.

He started the car and headed for the café. Khalil turned on every ounce of charm he possessed, and after fussing for a full five minutes and threatening him with bodily harm if he hurt Lexia again, Sam relented and gave him the address.

He stopped by the gym to let Cam and Felicia know he

would be gone for a couple of days. As he was leaving, his phone buzzed with a text message.

Hey, bro. Just left the mayor's office. He promised to help expedite all the paperwork for the building permits so we can get this project off the ground.

Khalil chuckled. He wanted to ask how Brandon had gotten on the mayor's calendar so quickly and secured the man's help, but knew how relentless his brother could be. His siblings had picked up the ball and taken care of business. Malcolm had reached out and found two buses and the renovations had already started. If they could find drivers, the mobile services could potentially be up and running in a month. The building would take longer to refit.

As he drove home to pack, Khalil turned his attention back to winning Lexia over. He planned to pull out all the stops. A smile curved his mouth. He engaged the Bluetooth in his car and reached out to an old friend for help. His fear notwithstanding, it was time for him to put all his cards on the table.

Chapter 19

Khalil leaned against the side of the beachfront house and observed Lexia sitting near the water and letting the sand drift through her hands. She wore a long-sleeved T-shirt, sweatpants and tennis shoes. His heart nearly beat out of his chest with the sheer magnitude of his emotions. He loved this beautiful and unique woman and had been a fool to let her go. He stood there a few moments longer to gather his courage, then straightened and sauntered over to where she sat.

Lexia startled and jumped away. "*Khalil?* What are you doing here?"

He wanted to kiss her, badly, but didn't think it would go over too well right now. He removed his shades so he could have an unobstructed view of the face that had haunted him for the past two weeks. The only difference was her eyes. In them, he saw sadness and a hint of fire. "I came to talk to you."

"The only person who knew my whereabouts was Sam, so I'm assuming the traitor told you," Lexia said with a roll of her eyes.

He chuckled. "She did, but not before threatening to gut me with the sharpest knife in the café and promising that I'd never get another piece of coffee cake if I hurt you again."

She fixed her eyes on a bird flying overhead and a small smile crossed her lips. When she faced him again, it was gone. "So, did you take her threats seriously?"

"I did. But not because I'm worried about being gutted or not having the coffee cake." Khalil paused. "Well, maybe I'm a *little* concerned about the coffee cake," he said with a smile. "Honestly, I'm far more worried about hurting you."

Lexia looked away. "And you did."

A pang of regret hit him. He sighed heavily and turned her face toward his. "Baby, I know I hurt you. Please believe me when I say I am *truly* sorry. I love you, Lexia."

She gasped softly and surprise filled her face. Just as quickly, the wariness came back. "I don't think this is a good idea, Khalil." She rose to her feet.

He gently took her hand. "Please don't leave. Give me a chance to explain."

She stared at him for a long moment, and then dropped back down onto the sand next to him.

"Thank you." Khalil didn't let go of her hand, held it tighter to draw from her strength. He closed his eyes to block out the images. He opened them again and met Lexia's expectant gaze. He lowered his head. "Her name is Michaela Phillips. And because of her, I spent thirty-six hours in an overcrowded, dirty prison in Mexico."

"Oh my God," Lexia whispered.

"We'd been dating for about a year and were on a modeling assignment together. I had planned to propose to her the day our photo shoot ended and, instead, was arrested at a restaurant with her and another four models and locked up with no explanation. They took my watch, the engagement ring that was in my pocket and every dime I had in my wallet." The memories rose so sharply he could almost smell the foul stench of unwashed bodies, urine, feces and rotten food. "I heard bits and pieces of their conversation and realized it had to do with drugs."

"Wait. How did you know what they were saying? Do you understand Spanish?"

Khalil smiled. "*Sí, y puede hablar con soltura.* Yes, and can speak fluently. French, as well."

Lexia's mouth fell open.

"Anyway, after several hours, they finally told me I was being held on drug trafficking charges. I was twenty-five years old and had never even gotten a traffic violation. I tried to tell them over and over that I had no idea what they were talking about, but…"

Lexia entwined their fingers. "What happened?"

"Apparently Michaela and two other models were using their assignments to distribute cocaine. They'd been under investigation for a while and had made another drop the evening before, only this time to undercover agents."

"I'm so sorry." She scooted closer and laid her head against his shoulder. "How did you get out?"

"My agent. He'd been looking for me because we were scheduled to have dinner with some dignitaries and I never showed. He went to the police, showed them my picture and found out I was in custody. Fortunately for me, during the times the deals went down, I had airtight alibis, including the previous night—my agent and I were having dinner with a high-ranking government official—and they had to let me go." Khalil fell silent. "You're the only one who knows."

Lexia wrapped an arm around his waist. "Why didn't you tell your family? After meeting them, I know they would have come for you."

"I don't know. Pride. Humiliation. I didn't want them to worry." When Khalil returned home two days later, he had done his best to act normal. He had also decided to retire from modeling the following year, an announcement that had shocked his family. "I promised myself that I would never let another woman get close to me again." He shifted until he was facing Lexia. "Then you came along. From the moment we met, I knew there was something different about you." *She may not be the type you're used to dating, but she may end up being* exactly *your type.* He heard Brandon's words in his mind and had to admit that this time his brother had been right. "I want and need you in my life, Lexia. Can we start again?"

She stared out at the water, seemingly considering his offer. "How do I know you won't hurt me again?"

"You don't," he said softly. "Just like I don't know if you'll hurt me. My mother told me that there is always a risk when it comes to love, but the payoff is worth it." He leaned closer and brushed his lips against hers. "Take the risk with me, baby. I promise to make every moment worth it."

A tear ran down her cheek and she nodded. "I love you, Khalil."

Khalil wiped the tear away and smiled. "I know." He captured her mouth in a tender and healing kiss infused with everything overflowing in his heart. *Now I'm happy.*

Lexia tore her mouth away and slanted him a curious glance. "What do you mean, you know?"

"You said it that night in New York. I had been hearing muffled snippets for a couple of days, but yours were the first clear words in my ear. And, like a fool, I ran from them. But I'm not running anymore."

She placed her palm on his cheek. "I didn't want you to hear them because I wanted to run, too."

As always, her touch did something to him. "No more running…for either of us."

"No more running."

Khalil kissed her once more, shifted her until she was between his legs and wrapped his arms around her. Contentment unlike anything he had ever experienced filled him and it came to him that he could sit with her this way for the rest of his life. For the first time, the thought of permanency with a woman didn't evoke the fear that had ruled his life for the past eight years. Sam had told him that Lexia planned to stay here until Sunday, which meant he had two days to convince her to marry him.

At length, Lexia asked, "How long are you staying?"

"As long as you are, hopefully."

She whipped her head around. "You booked a hotel?"

"Not yet. Do I need to?"

"Of course not. This house has four bedrooms and there are plenty to choose from."

"Then I choose whichever bed you'll be in." Her mouth fell open and he burst out laughing. Khalil tickled her ribs. "You thought you were being slick, huh?"

Lexia squealed with laughter and squirmed to get away from him. "Stop it, crazy man!" She slapped at his hands.

Soon they were both laughing. She knocked him backward in the sand, straddled his waist and managed to do the same to him before he pinned her arms and started to roll over.

She stopped laughing. "If you get sand in my hair, you're going to be sleeping in your car."

He flipped onto his back. "Since you put it that way."

"What am I going to do with you?"

He lifted a brow.

An embarrassed expression crossed her face. "That's not what I mean, and you know it."

Khalil's body didn't care. He wanted to make love to her here and now, but reined in his impatience. They had the next two days and he needed her to know that he wanted more for them than just sex. He prayed he could last at least one day.

Saturday morning, Lexia squinted at the sunlight streaming through the partially open curtains. The heat behind her reminded her that she wasn't alone. Carefully shifting, her gaze roamed over the gorgeous man asleep next to her. Khalil's showing up had definitely been a surprise, but she couldn't be mad at him—or Sam. Sam had made her position clear and Lexia knew her best friend would do anything to see Lexia happy, even if it meant being sneaky.

She resisted the urge to trail her fingers over Khalil's face and down his magnificent bare chest visible above the sheet. Her heart went out to him for what he had endured for that day and a half. He'd told her about fighting to protect himself, the fear of not knowing whether he'd be released, not getting his belongings back and isolating himself from virtually everyone for a short while. That he chose to reveal the truth to her only made her love him more. She had been blown away by the fact that he knew Spanish and French. The way the words rolled off his tongue in that sexy voice had her wanting to strip him naked and straddle him right there on the beach. They had spent Friday talking, walking along the beach, watching movies and finding their way back to each other. She felt them growing closer and hoped that meant good things for their relationship.

Lexia had expected them to make love last night, but he had only kissed her, pulled her close and gone to sleep just like he'd done on Thursday. A part of her had been disappointed, but as he held her throughout the night, she'd been content. As if sensing her scrutiny, Khalil opened his eyes.

"Morning, beautiful."

"Good morning to you, too."

Khalil stretched. "What time is it?"

Lexia glanced over her shoulder at the clock on the nightstand. "Just after eight."

He fingered one of the braids he'd helped her do last night. "Think you can be ready to leave at nine so we can stop for a quick breakfast? We have a ten o'clock appointment."

She rose up on her elbow. "Where?"

A smile curved his lips. "It's a surprise." He tossed her a wink, flipped the covers back and slid off the bed.

She hopped off the bed and trailed him to the bathroom. "I know that's not all you're going to say."

"Unless you want to be late and miss your surprise, I suggest you leave the bathroom while you still can. If you stay one more minute, we *are* going to be late. You do remember the last time we were in the bathroom together?" he asked with a wicked grin.

Lexia remembered with exceptional clarity what happened in the shower at his gym. And so did her body. The way he was staring at her didn't help, either. But curiosity about what the surprise might be got the better of her and she backed out of the door.

Khalil chuckled. "We'll save it for later then."

"Whatever. Just hurry up and don't use all the hot water."

"No worries there," he mumbled. "I don't think I'll be needing the hot water."

Her gaze followed his down to his fully erect shaft straining against his briefs. If they made it quick...

"No, baby. As bad as I want you right now, we wouldn't have nearly enough time."

Lexia gripped the knob and pulled the door closed away from temptation. She heard Khalil's laughter as she flopped down on the bed to wait her turn and tried to figure out what he had up his sleeve.

An hour later, they were seated in a nearby family-owned restaurant. She ordered the breakfast burrito and Khalil had the egg white vegetable scramble. Not for the first time, she noticed that he had ordered a healthier meal option. *Probably why his body looked the way it did.*

While waiting for their food, she clasped her hands in front of her on the table. "So, this was the big surprise?"

Khalil leaned back in his chair and folded his arms. "Nope."

She narrowed her eyes. "What are you planning?"

"You'll have to wait and see."

"You just got here two days ago and we've been together the whole time. How did you have time to plan whatever this is?"

He merely smiled.

"I can't believe you aren't going to tell me." Lexia batted her eyes sweetly. "If you tell me, I'll *totally* make it worth it." Desire leaped into his eyes and for a moment, she thought he would relent.

He shook his head. "Nah, baby. It's not going to work. And stop pouting," he added with a chuckle. "This is our last day here and I just want us to have some special time together. Trust me?"

Lexia had never been really comfortable with surprises, mainly because most times they didn't end well. But she assured herself that this time would be different. He'd confessed to loving her and they'd spent the last couple of days talking openly about their hopes and fears, so she would trust him. "Yes."

Their food arrived and, while eating, they talked about what he would do if he didn't regain hearing in his right ear and the mobile services and transitional housing projects for the homeless that he'd started.

"I can't believe you did all that in two weeks."

"You met Brandon, so you know how forceful he can be. We're always telling him to chill, but in this instance, it's working in our favor, so it's all good."

Lexia smiled. The image of his brother standing over the paramedic glaring and remembering how he'd manipulated her floated through her mind. "I know what you mean." She couldn't wait to see the converted buses and thought that a novel idea. Once they were done, Khalil settled the bill and escorted her out to the car. Five minutes later, he pulled into the lot at San Ysidro Ranch. The upscale resort was highly rated and known for its luxury, natural beauty and romantic heritage. "Um…we already have a place to stay. You do not need to waste good money on a hotel."

Khalil hopped out of the car and came around to help her out. "We're not staying here. And even if we were, I wouldn't consider spending my money on you a waste. You're worth every penny I have and more. I'd give it all away if it meant having you in my life." He placed a lingering kiss on her lips.

If she didn't already love him, that statement would have pushed her over the edge. "You are…" Her emotions swelled. She placed her hand on his chest and felt the strong, steady beat of his amazing heart.

"And so are you. Come on, sweetheart."

Inside, Lexia found out that he had arranged for them to have a couples' massage, and then left her to be further pampered with a facial, manicure and pedicure. By the time Khalil came back for her, she was totally relaxed. She wrapped her arms around him and laid her head on his chest. "Thank you so much. This was the best surprise I've ever had."

"You're welcome. Hungry?"

"A little." It had been almost five hours since breakfast. Over her protests, he escorted her to the hotel's restaurant and they had a light lunch at a price that widened her eyes.

Afterward, they played tourists and took a scenic tour of Santa Barbara. They even stopped at a park and played on the swings like kids. It was the best date she'd ever had, hands down, and she wished she could spend the rest of her life with him, just this way.

Chapter 20

Dusk had fallen by the time they got back to the house. Lexia started up the walkway and stopped when she realized he was still standing by the car. "Are you coming?"

"Yeah. I just need to get something out of the car." Khalil rounded the car and popped the trunk. "Go on in. I'll be there in a minute."

"Okay." Lexia paused at the sight of a note on the door. She walked closer and read: *A house of love...* "What does that mean?" she mumbled and stuck her key in the door. She opened it and froze. Her hands flew to her mouth and tears filled her eyes. *"Oh my."* Roses of every shade covered the room. Some were in vases, while others had been placed on chairs and tables. She glanced up and saw that a few had even been affixed to the ceiling.

"What do you think?"

She whirled around at the sound of Khalil's voice. "It's amazing, beautiful, *unbelievable*." He must have come back to the house while she was at the spa. She walked farther into the room, still in shock. Beneath her feet, red rose petals had been placed in what appeared to be a path. She glanced over her shoulder at Khalil. "Does this lead somewhere?"

"Yes."

Lexia tentatively continued, trying to look ahead to see where it ended. When she got to the back deck, the tears spilled over. The roses continued onto the deck, and then were replaced with a path of candles that ended at an elegantly set table for two on the beach. She looked up at him. "I have never met anyone like you, Khalil Gray. I love you."

Khalil lowered his head and placed a tender kiss on her lips. "And I love you." He took her by the hand, led her to the table and seated her. Then he pulled out his phone, made a call and took the seat adjacent to her.

Only then did she notice that a mock band stage had been set up a short distance away. "Did you…?"

He grinned. "I asked an old friend if he could help me out." He pointed behind her.

She nearly fell out of her chair. "Is that *Monte*? *He's* your old friend? Ohmigod! I *love* his music. This is fantastic!" She slapped a hand over her mouth to stop rambling like a crazy fangirl, but couldn't stop bouncing in her chair.

He laughed and shook his head. "You never get that excited when you see me."

She patted his hand. "Aw, you know I love you, baby."

Monte and another man reached the table and Khalil stood to embrace each man. "Thanks for helping me out."

Monte smiled and clapped Khalil on the back. "No problem."

Khalil gestured to Lexia. "I'd like you to meet Lexia Daniels. Lexia, this is Terrence Campbell, or Monte, and Donovan Wright, his best friend and manager."

Lexia couldn't get her mouth to work. She shook herself and extended her hand. "Sorry for staring like a starstruck kid, but I'm a big fan. It's really nice to meet you both. Do you prefer Terrence or Monte?"

Terrence shook her hand. "It's a pleasure to meet you, Lexia. Terrence is fine."

Donovan repeated the gesture. "Nice to meet you, Lexia. So how did you meet this clown?" he asked, pointing at Khalil.

She laughed. "Over a slice of low fat apple cinnamon coffee cake and a cup of tea in my café. He was very persistent."

Terrence nodded. "Hey, that's the only way to get your girl."

The three men did fist bumps and Lexia rolled her eyes. She knew that Terrence and Donovan had both gotten married a few years ago and had two children each. Lexia opened her mouth to say something, but was interrupted by the arrival of two men pushing a cart with what she assumed was their dinner.

"That's my cue," Terrence said. "Any requests, Lexia?"

She really wanted to ask him to sing every song on every one of his eight CDs, but figured that wouldn't be practical. "Can you sing 'Just To Be With You' and 'It's Only You'?"

"Absolutely." He inclined his head. "Enjoy your dinner." He and Donovan sauntered off and joined the band.

Lexia faced Khalil. "I know I said earlier that this was the best surprise ever, but this…this is…" She swiped at the tears and chuckled. "I have never been this emotional. You're ruining my tough girl image."

Khalil leaned over and kissed the escaped tear. "I want you to know how much you mean to me."

They dined on mixed green salads, seared scallops in a white wine sauce, steamed vegetables and the fluffiest mashed potatoes that Lexia had ever eaten. The band played instrumental versions of Monte's songs as the sun set in an explosion of purple, orange and pink.

"Would you like anything else?" Khalil asked when she finished.

"No, thank you. Everything was delicious."

He placed his napkin on the table, stood and extended his hand. "Dance with me." He helped her to her feet and slid his arms around her.

Lexia laid her head on his chest and swayed to the slow beat as Monte sang the lyrics to her favorite songs. They danced to song after song. She still couldn't believe that she was being treated to a private concert with one of her favorite artists.

"Do you remember when I told you this wasn't a fairy tale?"

She lifted her head. "Yes."

"I lied." Khalil held her eyes. "This is a fairy tale of the most magical kind. What else could have brought you into my life? From the first time you touched me, I felt something different, something frightening...but in a good way. I finally figured out what it was."

"What was it?"

"Love. When you touch me, I feel love."

Lexia gasped softly. "I feel it, t—" She stopped abruptly when he lowered himself to one knee. She brought her hands to her mouth and her heart thumped in her chest. He opened a small velvet box and there was just enough light to see the solitaire surrounded by diamonds nestled inside.

"Lexia, you make me happier than I ever thought I could be. And, if you let me, I'll spend the rest of my life trying to make you feel the same way. Marry me, baby. Take the risk with me. I promise it'll be worth it."

"Yes, yes, *yes!*"

Khalil slid the ring onto her finger and signed, *I love you.* Lexia smiled and signed the same to him.

He swept her up in his arms and swung her around and around. "Thank you."

He covered her mouth in a drugging kiss and Lexia lost herself in the sensations. She forgot about the music, the food, everything—except him carrying her upstairs to the bedroom, where he made love to her with a tenderness that touched her very soul.

The next three weeks passed in a blur. Between his new gym's grand opening two weeks ahead of schedule and getting the other three projects up and running, it seemed like ages since Khalil and Lexia had spent some uninterrupted time together. He had hoped they would have time this weekend, but forgot about his family's picnic until his mother reminded him three days ago. His mother always held a barbecue the Saturday before Memorial Day. He longed for the quiet days of Santa Barbara and decided that at least once a month, he would steal Lexia away.

Khalil pulled up in front of the side-by-side hotels that would serve as housing and was pleased with the progress.

"This is going to be so nice," Lexia said as he helped her out of the car.

"When it's done, we'll have space for up to fifty men, women and families. It would be more, but because we wanted to include families, some of the units need to be larger." They walked around the side where the two buses were parked. He unlocked the shower one first and gestured her inside. The bus had three stalls, each closed off with a door—affording the person privacy when getting undressed and dressed—three sinks and cabinets filled with towels, bath supplies and cleaning supplies.

"I just can't get over how cool this is." She turned in a slow circle.

"Come on. Let me show you the other one." He locked the bus and went to the next one.

Lexia climbed the steps and peered down the aisle. "Wow." She pointed. "So, these cooler bins will have fresh fruits and vegetables?"

"Yes, and some deli meats. There will also be bread, water, nuts, protein bars and other nonperishables." Khalil wished they could do more, but it was a start.

"And this bus will go to the designated neighborhoods once a week."

"Yeah. Our goal is for people to get at least a bag of groceries to last until the next visit."

She hugged him tight. "You guys are doing a good thing."

"The credit goes to you and Cameron," he said as he locked the door. "By the way, did he tell you the name he decided on?"

She leaned back. "No."

"He wants to call it The Janice Hughes Transitional Living Facility, after his late wife. I thought it only fitting that he got to choose the name, since much of this was his idea." Aside from being a great manager, Cameron had proven to be an astute businessman and had been instrumental in helping them find a place for the young man caring for his siblings. Brandon had offered him an internship at Grays, and would work around his school schedule, but still give him a steady income to provide for his high school brother and sister.

"Good grief. I've done more crying in the last month, than I've done in my entire life," she said with a little laugh as she wiped at her face. "It's a beautiful name."

He kissed her forehead. "As long as they're happy tears, I can deal with it." He glanced at his watch. "We'd better get going. My mother will have a fit if we're late." His mother had insisted on giving them an engagement party and to keep her from going over-the-top, he'd convinced her to combine it with their normal Memorial Day picnic. She had fussed for an hour before relenting. Khalil could imagine her outrage when he announced their wedding date.

"Well, come on. I don't want to get in trouble with your mother. And you know we have to pick up my parents from the hotel first." Lexia pulled him back around the front to the car.

"You'll be fine." Lexia's parents had arrived yesterday and after meeting her mother, he knew where Lexia had gotten her spunk. Mrs. Daniels had no problems grilling him over dinner with pointed questions, while her husband looked on with a smile. Apparently, he had passed the test because both gave their blessing in the end.

When they made it to his parents' house, Khalil's mother met them at the sliding glass door leading to the backyard.

"There you are. What took you so long?"

"Hey, Mom." He kissed her cheek. "It's not like we're late."

She sent a scowl his way. Then, smiling, she took Lexia's hands and kissed her cheek. "Hello, Lexia. I'm so happy to have you. These must be your parents." She turned when Khalil's dad approached.

"Hey, son. Lexia."

"Hey, Dad."

Lexia smiled. "It's good to see you, Mr. and Mrs. Gray. And, yes, these are my parents, Bobby and Petrina Daniels."

"I'm DeAnna and this is Nolan. It is such a pleasure to meet you. Your daughter is a jewel. Please, come in. Let me introduce you to everyone."

Khalil watched with a smile as his mother, ever the hostess, escorted the Danielses around. He slung an arm around Lexia's shoulder. "You want something to drink?"

"Not right now. I love your family. They're so warm and friendly."

"Yeah, they are." He considered himself blessed to have them.

He and Lexia talked, laughed, ate and played games with his siblings. Sam, Cameron, Jayla, Elyse and her husband, and Mr. Willis had also joined them.

After the food had been consumed, Khalil stood and sent a sharp whistle across the yard to get everyone's attention. "I'd like to make a couple of announcements." He waited until all eyes turned his way before continuing. "The first one is I'll be having surgery on Tuesday to repair the eardrum in my right ear." He had waited to tell his family to minimize all the drama and hovering he knew would follow. "Next, Lexia and I will be getting married the second weekend in September in Santa Barbara." She had fallen in love with the gardens at San Ysidro Ranch and he had taken the liberty of booking it before they left. It happened to be the only Saturday available for the remainder of the year. And he refused to wait another year to make her his wife.

"What?" His mother placed her hand on her hip. "That's barely three months away. Not enough time to plan anything."

"Hey, it's more time than when Siobhan and Justin got married." His sister had married six weeks after becoming engaged.

Laughter broke out.

Mrs. Daniels divided a glance between Khalil and Lexia. "What's the big rush? Are you pregnant, Lexia?"

Lexia dropped her head in her hands and shook her head. "No, Mom. I am not. This was the only date available before winter."

While the two mothers continued to fuss, Khalil gathered his future wife into his arms and kissed her with a passion that silenced the onlookers. Despite what their mothers wanted, he wasn't going to wait one day past the date they had set to make Lexia his.

Epilogue

Three months later...

Khalil stood on the estate lawn with his brothers and brothers-in-law waiting for his wedding to begin. They couldn't have picked a more perfect day. The sun shone overhead in a clear blue sky, the temperature hovered at a comfortable seventy-five and they had a magnificent view of the ocean.

Brandon placed a hand on Khalil's shoulder. "How are you feeling?"

"I'm fine, Brandon." His brother had asked him the question virtually every week since the surgery. So far, Khalil had regained only 30 percent hearing in his right ear. The doctor said it could take up to a year to determine a true measure, but just being able to hear again was enough for Khalil right now.

"You ready to do this, little brother?"

"I am. Been ready. You know, Malcolm, you're going to be the only single man standing in about forty-five minutes. If you need some pointers, let us know." They all chuckled.

Malcolm glared at Khalil. "You're lucky it's your wedding day, otherwise I'd tell you what you could do with that statement. I plan to be a bachelor for *life*. I'm not letting another woman run roughshod over my heart ever again," he added through clenched teeth.

Khalil sighed. He knew what his brother meant and remembered when Malcolm's college sweetheart broke his heart. "If I can find love after what happened to me, you can, too."

All heads swung his way and Brandon asked, "What are you talking about?"

Before he could answer, the music started and the minister asked them to take their places. He smiled as his brothers escorted his and Lexia's mother to their seats. Both women looked gorgeous in champagne-colored sequined gowns. Next came his sisters, Sam, and Elyse. Finally, Lexia came toward him on the arm of her father wearing a stunning white satin creation that caressed her every curve. She had her hair up like she'd done when they were in New York. His heart rate kicked into high gear and it took everything in him to stand still.

Brandon whispered, "Remember how much grief you gave me when I kissed Faith before the minister uttered one word? Well, you have the same look on your face, so let's see how much of that legendary control you always brag about you have now."

Brandon was dead-on, but Khalil wouldn't give his brother the satisfaction of saying so. He could control himself. He had the rest of his life to kiss her. But when Lexia reached him, turned to hand her bouquet to Sam and he saw the sheer back of her gown with the lace detail and tiny buttons running down the center and the same shoes she'd worn in New York, he almost lost it.

Lexia faced him.

"The tiara is a nice touch," he told her with amusement.

She gave him a sultry smile. "You said it was a fairy tale. I'm just playing my part."

"And you're playing it very well. Remember what happened the last time you wore a dress like this? And those sexy shoes?"

She narrowed her eyes. "Don't you dare even think about it."

Khalil grinned. "Whatever you say." Smiling, she shook her head and they turned toward the minister. They repeated their vows and, as promised, Terrence sang her favorite song, "It's Only You." After the ceremony and posing for a million pictures, Khalil swept Lexia into his arms and strode down the rose-strewn pathway.

"Where are you going?"

"To the cottage I reserved."

Lexia's mouth fell open. "Cottage? You can't do that. What about the reception? People are going to wonder when we don't show up."

He gazed down at her. "I never said we weren't going to show up. The meal won't be served for another forty-five minutes and there are enough drinks and snacks to keep the guests busy. That's plenty of time for a little taste of what's coming later."

She stared at him as if he was crazy. "It took me longer than forty minutes to get this dress on. And—"

"Then we'll leave it on. And, yeah, I know...don't mess up your hair." Khalil unlocked the cottage door, carried her over the threshold and lowered her to her feet.

"You are outrageous."

"You ain't seen nothing yet, baby." His hands went to his belt. "I'm going to show you just how outrageous I can be."

She slid her palms over his chest. "Well, if you insist." She came up on tiptoe and pulled his head down for a deep, soul-stirring kiss.

Just like the first time she touched him and every time since, he felt it. Love. He had risked it all and this time, he'd won. And as he told her, he would spend the rest of his life proving to her that they were worth it.

* * * * *

Don't miss Malcolm Gray's story,
STILL LOVING YOU
coming in April 2018!

And catch up with the rest of Sheryl Lister's
THE GRAYS OF LOS ANGELES series:

GIVING MY ALL TO YOU
PLACES IN MY HEART
TENDER KISSES

Available now from Harlequin Kimani Romance!

COMING NEXT MONTH
Available November 21, 2017

#549 SEDUCED BY THE TYCOON AT CHRISTMAS
The Morretti Millionaires • by Pamela Yaye

Italy's most powerful businessman, Romeo Morretti, spends his days brokering multimillion-dollar deals, but an encounter with Zoe Smith sends his life in a new direction. When secrets threaten their passionate bond, Romeo must fight to clear his name before they can share a future under the mistletoe.

#550 A LOVE LIKE THIS
Sapphire Shores • by Kianna Alexander

All action star Devon Granger wants for Christmas is a peaceful escape to his hometown. How is he to rest with Hadley Monroe tending to his every need? And when the media descends on the beachfront community, their dreams of ringing in the New Year together could be out of their grasp…

#551 AN UNEXPECTED HOLIDAY GIFT
The Kingsleys of Texas • by Martha Kennerson

When a scuffle leads to community service, basketball star Keylan "KJ" Kingsley opts to devote his hours to his family's foundation. Soon he plunges into a relationship with charity executive Mia Ramirez. When KJ returns to the court, will his celebrity status risk the family that could be theirs by Christmas?

#552 DESIRE IN A KISS
The Chandler Legacy • by Nicki Night

On impulse, heir to a food empire Christian Chandler creates a fake dating profile and quickly connects with petite powerhouse Serenity Williams. She's smart, down-to-earth and ignites his fantasies from their first encounter. But how can he admit the truth to a woman for whom honesty is everything?

KPCNM1117

Get 2 Free Books,
Plus 2 Free Gifts—
just for trying the Reader Service!

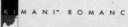

LOVE
Harlequin
romance?

Join our Harlequin community to share your thoughts and connect with other romance readers!

Be the first to find out about promotions, news, and exclusive content!

Sign up for the Harlequin e-newsletter and download a free book from any series at

www.TryHarlequin.com

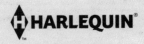